Secret Body

Published by Preacher's Kid Productions
Santa Monica, CA 90405
www.preacherskidproductions.com

Dedication

In loving memory of my greatest fan: Ruth Mae Crawford.

Chapter One

The monkey was ticking.

Trevor Cole frowned at the furry electric blue animal he'd just picked up with his right hand. The gaudy thing was wearing a purple top hat and had the nerve to grin at him all while squeezing out soft ticks that marked each second.

At first glance, the monkey appeared harmless enough. The most apparent danger seemed to be limited to its extreme ugliness. Although if he stared at it long enough, he figured he might start to see it as cute. And that's what had Trevor removing the monkey from its unassuming box for a closer inspection. No sooner had he picked it up, than he'd felt something snap followed by the steady ticks that shredded his nerves with each passing moment that could very well be his last.

Needing to calm himself, Trevor closed his eyes and took a long, slow breath like he would before going onstage. He needed a clear head if this latest present was indeed what it sounded like it was. Trevor opened his eyes, refusing to even acknowledge the jolt of fear that seized his heart. He addressed his driver from where he sat motionless in the understated Lincoln Town Car's back seat. He was careful to keep his grip steady on the squishy little monkey body that just filled his palm.

"We need to swing by the police station. Immediately."

The man spared Trevor a look in the rear view mirror. "No can do, boss. You put me under strict orders to take you straight to the mansion. You have that song to finish, and I'm not supposed to let you keep procrastinating."

"Not to alarm you, but I think the monkey is a bomb. I'm pretty sure I activated it when I picked it up."

Trevor watched the big man's eyes widen in alarm. His large beefy hands gripped the steering wheel so tight Trevor was convinced that it would snap in two. Trevor hired the man in part because of those big hands. He had no trouble keeping a line of determined fans in check. Doubtless it didn't hurt that those hands were attached to six foot nine, two hundred and seventy five pounds of solid muscle. Trevor figured hiring a guy who looked like him would get his best friend off his back about his lax security. What does a musician need with top of the line protection anyway? Talk about ego. Trevor conveniently ignored the monkey for the duration of that line of reasoning.

"Dude. Why'd you pick it up?"

"Not the most pressing issue at the moment."

"Can you see how much time we have?"

Trevor frowned. "Let's just get to the police station. They'll handle it."

The bodyguard shook his head. "I didn't sign up for this. You said someone was playing pranks on you. Not trying to kill you."

"We don't know this isn't a prank." He struggled to hold his voice steady and even while he tried to convince himself of this along with his driver.

Trevor fought to keep his balance when the bodyguard slammed on the brakes. The car skidded to a halt in the middle of a busy intersection. Drivers behind them honked at their audacity of stopping at a perfectly good green light.

"What are you doing?" Trevor asked, thankful the jolt hadn't set off the monkey.

The bodyguard turned and glared at Trevor. "I have a wife and kids, man."

With that, the guy threw open his door and fled. Trevor

watched in shock and some admiration at the speed with which a man of his size disappeared. Some bodyguard. He could forget about a final paycheck. Kids or not. Maybe a partial . . . Trevor shook his head. He had to get moving. Just in case he was holding the real thing this time.

Trevor unbuckled his seatbelt and inched from the backseat, careful not to disturb the monkey. He held his hand in place inside the vehicle until he'd gotten his body outside and stable. Not the easiest thing to do while his heart was thrumming a mile a minute. He was never one for sixth senses or whatnot, but something was starting to tell him that this was the real thing this go round.

Sweat beaded on his forehead when other motorists honked and swerved around him. Trevor flattened himself against the car's door and cursed under his breath when some idiot in a truck drove by him with only inches to spare. He was relieved to feel anger take over his fear. He should try to hold on to that fury. He maneuvered behind the wheel just after the light turned red. Another round of angry honking ensued while Trevor fought to get the car in gear with his left hand then guided it from the intersection. It was all so surreal. One second he was thinking of ways to increase his business expenses to decrease his taxes, and the next . . .

It was an extraordinarily bad idea to walk inside the small police station with a ticking bomb in his hand. Trevor figured it was best they come to him. He eased the Town Car to a halt in the Authorized Vehicles Only parking lot. Using his available hand, he fumbled his cell phone from his pocket, opened it, and hit a speed dial button. In his anger, he pressed on the phone just a bit too hard. He eased up when he heard it creak in protest.

Detective Cameron Dobbs answered on the second ring.

"Yo, Trev. Don't tell me Marcy called you already. I just hung up with her. She's expecting you for dinner this Saturday, but I suggest you invent other plans. She's dug up another date for you and—"

"Cam, I have a problem." Trevor looked toward the grated window he knew concealed his best friend's office.

"What's up?"

"I'm out back. I think somebody sent me a bomb, and I don't think I should put it down."

"Jeez, Trev. Stay put." The phone clicked when Cam hung

up.

Claustrophobic and more than a little fed up with the fear that was trying to take over, Trevor stepped from the car. Disgusted to see his hand trembling, he rested the monkey on the hood. There were people who handled this kind of thing every day. Without even batting an eye no less.

Within moments, the back door flew open. Four guys in bomb gear dashed out and swarmed him. Case in point. These guys were rushing toward danger, and not one of them was shaking in his government-issued boots. Seconds later, Trevor frowned when they wrapped him like an adult sized baby in some kind of bright yellow blanket and jammed a hat with a face shield on his head before starting to work on his still-exposed hand.

Trevor followed the team leader's terse instructions to the letter. Ten minutes after he'd pulled up, the monkey and his hand parted in peace. Trying to keep his shaky knees to himself, Trevor's stride was a bit stilted while he followed another officer inside the station. Cam was waiting just inside the door, a thunderous look on his hard, aristocratic face. He thumped his wheelchair down on all four wheels to face Trevor head-on. Trevor avoided his angry stare by concentrating on shucking the protective gear.

"What kind of bodyguard doesn't check your packages first?" Cam looked around. "Where is that big goof anyway?"

"He sort of took off when I told him what it was." In vain, Trevor plucked at his sweat stained shirt and worked up the nerve to look Cam in the eye. He sniffed and then noticed a uniformed officer escorting an unkempt prisoner past them. Trevor hoped with fervor that the sudden stench came from the man and not him. Though he wasn't about to lay odds on it.

"What the . . . where'd you find that idiot anyway? The phone book?" Cam asked, interrupting Trevor's assessment of the other stinky dude.

Trevor looked at Cam, but couldn't quite meet his eyes while he searched for a way to change the subject so he wouldn't have to admit that was just what he'd done. When his friend popped up on his back wheels again, Trevor knew that Cam had read his silence for what it was—confirmation.

"That's it. I'm getting you a bodyguard myself. Today." Cam spun in his chair, and rolled off into his office. Trevor chased after him.

"Hey, Cam, it's not necessary. We still don't know that the thing was a bomb. Besides, I am capable of taking care of myself." Which is why he refused to have a staff to wait on him hand and foot. Hiring the type of bodyguard he knew Cam would insist he have would start him down the slippery slope of everything he hated about stardom.

A muffled bang reverberated from the parking lot. Startled, the men looked toward the door. After a moment, Cam turned to level an irritated scowl at Trevor that dared him to try the whole prank argument again before picking up the phone to dial. Trevor scowled back to show he wasn't intimidated and watched Cam's fingers jab the numbers on a dial pad that had seen better years. Suspicions confirmed, Trevor hit the switch hook.

"Absolutely not. This is not worth Trecam's time."

Cam stared Trevor down. "Protecting the guy who funds their operation is not worth their time? You've lost your mind."

"I just think Caitlyn and crew have better things to do than follow around some so called celebrity who might have an issue. Besides, the police are more than capable of taking care of this." Trevor watched Cam's chest expand with pride at the mention of his fellow brothers in blue. Even though he was co-owner of one of the top security firms in the world, Detective Cameron Dobbs was first and foremost a cop. Trevor wasn't above using that knowledge to his full advantage to get what he wanted. Or what he didn't want and that was Trecam's involvement. Seeing his ploy taking effect, Trevor sank onto the ratty couch Cam kept in his otherwise immaculate office.

"Given the time, we can get to the bottom of this. But I worry that you're running out of it." Leveling a narrowed gaze on his friend, Cam replaced the phone receiver in its cradle. Trevor knew the man had just put him under the microscope of his keen detective skills so he fought to relax his posture and put a little flip in his tone. There was no way Trevor was going to give him even the smallest inkling that he couldn't handle this stalker situation or whatever it was without Trecam.

"I'm going on tour soon. I'll be out of reach. You'll have all the time you need." At least that's what Trevor hoped. He wouldn't give voice to his concerns. If he did, Cam would have Caitlyn on the line in two seconds flat. Once that happened, Trecam would be on the case whether he wanted them or not. Besides Caitlyn, no one even knew there were three founders instead of one. Given Trevor's high profile occupation, Caitlyn and Cam had refused to expose his involvement with the Firm. It would make him too much of an attractive target for their adversaries. Truth be told, staying in the background of this security venture suited Trevor just fine. Too much of his life was already public. He kinda liked having a secret.

"If you remember, we didn't go to any great lengths to hide our affiliation with the agency. You really want one of their agents poking around in my life because he's bored? These are people adept at finding the unfindable. It would be short work to figure out I'm the Tre in Trecam." Trevor sat forward to press home his point. "Then you, my friend, are going to find yourself back on the couch."

Cam's wife, Marcy, had enough to worry about with him being a cop. She'd kicked him out of their bed until he'd pulled his name off Trecam's official masthead. Still, all someone had to do was pull the right thread and the whole truth would come tumbling out. Trevor was not about to give any of Trecam's agents the opportunity to find those threads because they were bored babysitting him.

He was counting on Cam buying into his line of reasoning. If he did, he wouldn't probe into Trevor's real reason for not wanting Trecam involved. Cam would think he was nuts. Still, he couldn't shake the feeling that having Trecam on the case would be as good as buying him a ticket on the pampered, but hated celebrity express. That was the one thing Trevor was determined to never be.

"I'm going to see if they have any questions for me and then I'm heading home," Trevor announced when he stood. Cam raked a hand through his close-cropped, sunset red hair, making it stand up at all kinds of unnatural angles. He surprised Trevor by not raising any further objections.

"A piece of advice?" Cam wheeled out from behind his desk to follow Trevor to the door. "Never make a cell phone call while holding a bomb. It can detonate."

Trevor blanched. He needed a little levity. Immediately. "How about I just never hold a bomb again? That sounds like a better plan."

A grin blossomed on Cam's face, and he slapped Trevor on the back.

"About Saturday, Marcy's keeping this one under wraps so I can't screen her for you."

Trevor grimaced. "That sounds like a bad sign."

"Believe me, it is."

"Tell you what. I'll host a party on the yacht this Saturday. Marcy can bring her there. See if she's confident of herself around the groupies and hangers-on. If not, you can point out to Marcy that the mystery lady won't be comfortable adjusting to my lifestyle. Win-win."

Trevor and Cam pounded fists and shared a conspiratorial grin.

"Sounds like a plan. Later." Cam wheeled around in his chair and rolled off while Trevor headed off the way he'd come in so many times.

* * * *

A junior bomb tech almost ran over Cam in his haste to get to his team leader. "Sorry, sorry."

"What's the rush?" Cam studied the rookie's reddening face.

"We got the visual results on the Cole bomb. There was just enough Semtex in it to damage a hand. Wouldn't have killed him though. The rest was play dough." The recruit's expression filled with irritation. "Who does that? If you're going to the trouble of building a bomb, at least try to kill the target."

Cam fought to keep his own expression neutral. "Don't you have results to deliver?" The recruit took off.

When Cam settled behind his desk, a photo of him and Trevor when they were boys and standing by a creek caught his attention. They were grinning from ear to ear and holding up a tiny minnow like it was a Great White. Cam tore his gaze from the photo and tried to concentrate on the stack of files in front of him. Nothing penetrated his brain except for how close he'd come to losing his best friend today. Sleeping on the couch didn't sound any worse than not having Trevor around anymore. He was willing to risk it. Besides, Marcy would understand.

Cam picked up the phone and dialed. He drummed an impatient rhythm with his fingers on his desk.

"Caitlyn? It's Cam. Call me when you get this message. I don't care how late it is."

* * * *

Erica Kellogg sliced through the heated water of the Olympic-sized pool. She loved her morning swims. In particular, she loved it when the stars were still dazzling even in the predawn hours. Moments like these made her grateful for her career choice. It had never even crossed her mind before her swimming career had come to such an abrupt end, but everything had worked out for the best. Even while the thought passed through her consciousness, a little niggle of doubt sprouted. Erica ripped it out and focused on the plush headquarters that not only offered a state of the art workout facility, but also the just as modern pool Erica was enjoying on the building's roof at present. Seemed to her, she got more use out of it than anyone else, but she wasn't going to complain.

She would save her complaints for less trivial issues, like the fact that she'd completed her last assignment a good five days ago. She was ready and eager for action. Alas, things were just too slow at the moment. They hadn't gotten wind of any good assassination plots. No one had been kidnapped. There wasn't even any decent espionage happening. What was the world coming to?

Erica sputtered in disgust while she did a front walkover and then bodyrolled up to an eggbeater. Her powerful legs churned the water, propelling her sideways toward the pool's wall.

Once she reached the side, she sank just below the surface of the deep water in a crouch to prep for a boost. Erica burst upward and raised both arms over her head then sank back to her prep position. When she surfaced for the fifth boost, she was surprised to see that her boss had materialized on the deck. Even after five and half years, Erica still marvelled at how Caitlyn was able to move between points A and B in effect undetected.

"I have an assignment for you," Caitlyn said with no preamble. Erica was used to that. She'd never heard her boss waste even one word.

Erica couldn't keep the excitement out of her voice. She must be going solo on this one. If she weren't, her partner would be with her or she'd be filling her in instead of Caitlyn. "Who is it? A foreign dignitary? I heard Ambassador—"

"Trevor Cole. You've heard of him."

Erica noted that Caitlyn's last words were a statement not a question. She couldn't blame the woman. Who hadn't heard of Trevor Cole? Erica frowned while she pulled off her nose clip and tucked it in the bottom of her suit. "Wait a minute. He's known for his lax security, isn't he? Something about preferring freedom."

"Mr. Cole isn't asking for protection. In fact, he expressly asked that we steer clear of his case."

"Then why are we taking it?" Erica rested her goggles on her forehead to see her boss.

"He's a friend of a friend." Caitlyn's unwavering gaze had Erica dropping the remaining questions that had leapt into her mind. Must be a very good friend to have put that uncharacteristic line of worry on Caitlyn's smooth face. Hmm. Caitlyn and a rock star? It wasn't difficult for Erica to imagine.

Even though Caitlyn was a little older than she recalled reading Trevor was, Erica suspected the woman had a wild side. She couldn't help the speculation. It was all that wild sunset red hair Caitlyn worked to keep confined in a thick bun.

Shutting down her imagination, Erica refocused on the assignment. While she appreciated Caitlyn for trusting her to protect her "friend," the last thing Erica wanted was to be saddled with babysitting duty. Not when something much more interesting and more fun could pop up at any moment.

"Wouldn't a junior agent be better suited?"

"I need someone with your performance background. You're going in as the new addition to his show."

"I can't sing or dance or anything like that. What could I possibly do in his concerts?"

"Swim." Caitlyn set a stack of CDs on the deck. "I'll be back this afternoon to see what you've come up with. You're in the field tomorrow." With that last statement, Caitlyn turned on her sensible pump and strode away. Erica hoisted herself from the pool even while hope dared to blossom in her chest, and she picked up the pile of Trevor Cole music that had been left for her.

"I can't choreograph all this by the afternoon." But Erica's protest fell on no ears at all. Caitlyn was already gone.

Back at her homey condo with two CDs down, Erica

shocked herself to admit she enjoyed the quirky sense of humor that came through in Trevor's irreverent lyrics. Some brief Internet research told her he was indeed the songwriter, and it was as if she'd already begun to know him. But Erica wasn't about to rely on that. Besides, Caitlyn would provide a more in depth package later.

It took a little getting used to with its screaming guitar riffs and pounding bass, but once she made herself pay attention to the tracks, she started to appreciate his genius. She had never been all that into music. She'd heard a lot of songs because she'd enjoyed choreographing the routines to swim with her partner and became a master at picking the tunes that best suited them. Otherwise, Erica wasn't a sit and listen kind of girl. For the most part, she enjoyed silence.

She found the song that suited her to a T in the middle of the third CD. It started out with a pounding beat, slowed to a sultry country ballad in the middle and then jammed its way out. And, unlike its predecessors, it would be a snap to count. Erica repeated the song and experimented with some land drills. The choreography came to her with surprising ease. A couple more times through and she had a workable routine.

Despite what Caitlyn had implied, Erica knew her boss didn't expect her to make up routines to every song. Erica looked at the clock on her otherwise bare wall. She'd had enough time to grab a quick bite and get back to the pool where she could fine tune the routine. Erica converted the song to an MP3 and loaded it on her SwiMP3 player. Even though the pool was state of the art at her job, she was pretty sure it wasn't equipped with underwater speakers.

Erica stretched her lithe body while she considered costumes. It would be a hoot to give her boss the full synchro treatment. Before the notion could take root, Erica dismissed it. She should keep things simple. Besides, she hadn't even opened her trunk of costumes since she'd returned to the States. Intending to let the matter drop, Erica tried to turn away. Her feet had other plans. It was just a bunch of old swimsuits. What harm could there be in looking?

Almost without further contemplation, Erica slunk into her spare bedroom and slid the closet door open. She shook her head at the silliness of creeping around her own place. When she knelt by the trunk, it was like she was about to open Pandora's Box. Once she had, Erica wasn't sure how she'd ever be able to close it again.

Yet, she forged ahead. Erica lifted the heavy mahogany lid and waited for old ghosts to assail her. She blew out the breath she'd inadvertently held when they never came. She plunged a hand inside her past. A smile blossomed on her face when she sifted through old CDs and routines written and sealed in plastic bags.

She pushed it aside and pulled a garment bag free. Erica eased the zipper down to peer at the shiny, black costume she knew would be on top. Her smile slid away as she remembered the last time she'd worn the suit. Now that she'd let her guard down, the ghosts attacked.

Erica could never go back. Not after what she did. She'd even heard through her one remaining connection that her old duet partner had done a great job of keeping her on everyone's blacklist. Not that she could blame the woman.

Erica shook her memories away. She wasn't going to let the ghosts win. Not when she had the opportunity to swim again. And if she had to babysit a spoiled rock star who had some nervous nelly on his staff, then so be it.

Erica contemplated the costume still clenched in her fist. It was perfect for the assignment. The shiny leather-like polyester and the crystals her duet partner had placed inside the black netting with such care gave it a Dangerous Beauty kind of look Erica knew would complement the Trevor Cole song she'd chosen. Since she wasn't known for her imperfection, Erica had to wear it. With any luck, the ghosts would drown.

After lunch, Erica raced back to the pool to put the finishing touches on the choreography. She was thankful that her job required her to stay in shape. Otherwise, she'd have never made it through the routine that she had loaded with hybrids, spins and boosts, and had no choice but be impressive. Concerned with a section of the music where she was having trouble remembering the sequence, Erica climbed out of the water to lay on the sunny deck and land drill it.

She'd only gotten through it once and had screwed it up even more when a shadow fell over her.

"Cute suit."

Erica opened her eyes to see Caitlyn standing there. Erica

smiled and stood so her boss could also see the crystals running down the back of the suit. She wasn't expecting the whistles and catcalls from some of her coworkers who'd just joined them on the roof. Erica rolled her eyes at Jason who was still known as the office ladies' man even though his recent marriage had clipped his wings a bit.

"If I had known you'd fill out a suit like that, I'd have been first in line for your swim lessons."

Erica chuckled. When she'd joined the firm, she'd been surprised at how many of the agents couldn't swim. She'd taken it upon herself to give lessons twice a week. Even while on nearby assignments she had tried to make it in for the weekly lessons.

"I'm sure Katie would love that."

"Hey, I'm married. Not dead. She lets me admire every now and again," Jason said with a wolfish grin. A balled up jacket smacked him in the face. Erica laughed when Katie joined them on the pool deck with a couple of other smirking co-workers.

"Put your eyes back in your head, Markley," Katie teased while she slid an arm around his waist. Jason pulled her jacket off his face and gave her an innocent look.

"What? I was just sizing it up for you."

Katie laughed. "Whatever." She eyed Erica herself. "Although, I may change my mind. Girl, that is one gorgeous suit." Katie was a pixie compared to Erica's solid height. The suit would slide right off the poor woman.

"Thank you. It was made for me. I'm surprised it still fits."

"It fits," Jason remarked, but his eyes were locked on Katie.

Erica looked around the deck where no less than ten more of her colleagues had arrived. She shot a questioning look at Caitlyn.

"I thought you could use an audience."

"It'll be a little difficult to enjoy without the music." Erica shrugged. "I don't have a system."

Caitlyn's lips quirked in what would pass for a smile. "I do." She motioned for Erica to follow and strode over to the pump room. Erica was surprised to see a built-in sound system. "We added it once we were sure you were going to come aboard. I like to be prepared to fully use our agents' skills."

"In that case, give me three minutes and I'll give you the full show." Caitlyn nodded, and Erica handed over the CD she was going to use before scampering off to get her bag.

True to her word, in three minutes, Erica slammed the restroom door open and strutted out to the pool deck. Since she'd gelled her hair at her condo, all that had been left to do was to add heavy black eyeliner and mascara over a dark bronze shadow. A little color on her honey colored cheeks and caked on shiny bronze lipstick completed the character Erica had donned for the performance. She was pleased to note her co-workers' surprised expressions at her in-your-face appearance. Once she was positioned at the end of the pool, she nailed Caitlyn with a look and nodded for her to begin

the music. Her boss' normally expressionless face was also tinged with a little shock, but she turned on the CD. Erica smiled to herself and settled into her pose.

The music began.

Erica improvised her deck work and dove in the pool on the proper count. Her legs surfaced first while she executed a fast paced hybrid timed to perfection with the pounding beats. Lungs burning, she spun until her toes were under and tucked out of the vertical. Erica exploded out of the water in a boost that opened a powerful section of the music.

Erica muscled her way from one end of the pool to the other. Sometimes right side up. Most of the time, upside down. During the ballad that had hooked her, Erica disappeared under the water then walked her legs straight up in a vertical. When she had her upper thighs out of the water, she danced with her legs while using her support scull to travel across the pool. Halfway through the section, she surfaced for an arm sequence and was gratified to see her colleagues cheering for her. While she emoted with her arms, she looked each of her audience members in the eye, drawing them in.

The song changed to a forceful beat that would end the routine, and Erica's movements followed suit. Everything she did sharpened and became more distinct. She piked into another hybrid and her leg positions were just as precise. The song pounded toward its conclusion and so did Erica. When she struck the ending pose, thunderous applause sounded from the pool deck. Letting go of the character, Erica was humbled to see that more agents had taken a break from their jobs to watch her swim.

Erica spotted Caitlyn in the crowd and gave her a smile. "How's that?" Savoring the delicious adrenaline rush that she so very much longed for, she whip kicked to the edge of the pool.

Caitlyn clapped twice. High praise indeed. "I'll let the client know you're ready." Erica grinned and hoisted herself out of the water only to be swarmed with congrats. How she had missed this! The thrill of a perfect swim. Sharing what she could do with an audience. She still loved it. Maybe this assignment would be perfect after all. If this Trevor Cole guy got on her nerves, all she had to do was go underwater.

Once they were alone, Caitlyn picked up just like they'd never been interrupted. "It'll be up to you to convince him to use you in the show."

Erica's hand froze when she reached for her towel. "Wait a minute. I assumed that was already a done deal." Erica pictured her perfect assignment slipping from her grasp.

"Our contact is going to strongly suggest he add a new flavor to the show. You'll have to audition."

"How in the world am I supposed to arrange that? I kinda need a lot of equipment." Erica gestured at the pool and wrapped herself in the towel.

"Mr. Cole is hosting a party on his yacht Saturday night. I've gotten you an invite. You'll figure out how to audition there."

Erica fought to keep her face expressionless. A yacht pool couldn't be more than four, five feet deep tops. No way could she do her more impressive elements in such shallow water. The soaring enthusiasm building around the assignment took a sharp nosedive.

"What if I'm not what they're looking for?"

"You'll have to be. Mr. Cole's life depends on it." With that pronouncement Caitlyn strode for the building. She opened the door and then turned to look at Erica. "Just a reminder. Don't ever mention to Mr. Cole that you are his new bodyguard. And you've never heard of Trecam."

"I still don't understand why not." Erica snuggled into the towel to ward off the chill. She wasn't sure if it came from the light afternoon breeze or if it was her instincts warning her off this case.

"Let's just say that he doesn't believe our services are for him." After that puzzling little announcement, Caitlyn went inside leaving Erica alone on the roof with her musings. They were so troubling that Erica didn't even register that she had just seen her boss exit until a couple moments after the fact.

Chapter Two

Trevor was beginning to regret throwing this party. He looked around his yacht, bustling with partygoers, and didn't see a single familiar face. He didn't even see any interesting faces. His yacht was packed with big boobs, firm backsides and blank-faced bimbos. He'd stopped asking long ago how these random people always ended up at his parties and put it down to the nature of the beast.

He summoned up an interested smile for the big-chested chick talking his ear off about all the plastic surgeons she adored and plucked her full champagne glass from her fingers.

"Looks like you need a refill."

She giggled and simpered and brushed her impressive chest against him for what seemed like the millionth time. They didn't get any softer. In his opinion, she should get her money back. While he ambled away, he wondered if she'd had to relearn to walk after she'd acquired those monstrosities. If nothing else, he was extremely impressed she could keep her balance for such long periods of time.

He set their glasses down and glanced at the dock and was relieved to see Cam arrive with his wife, Marcy, both casual in jeans and T-shirts. His relief turned to surprise when he noticed that a pudgy woman seemed to be accompanying them. He took one look at her plaid flannel skirt with a high necked blouse and had to give her credit for being ballsy. Either she was deranged or she was so comfortable in her own skin that the silicon babes populating the party wouldn't bother her. Judging by her surprised reaction when a scantily clad chick flitted by, just avoiding the grasp of a muscle-bound surfer dude, Trevor didn't think it was the latter. While he studied her, he began to think that deranged might be a jump to a conclusion. She could just be a woman on a mission.

Trevor grimaced at the kind of mission the woman was on if she wasn't deranged.

Marcy couldn't expect the two of them to hit it off, could she? The woman had "Marry Me" written all over her. Right next to "wallflower." Having witnessed his parents' marriage firsthand, Trevor knew what he wanted in a wife. And wallflower was without a doubt not it. After his career took off, Trevor realized that a wallflower wouldn't stand for his lifestyle. Since he kinda liked the way things were with only a couple of exceptions, he wasn't about to get involved with someone who'd insist he'd change.

Before he could come up with more reasons to turn Marcy's friend down, Trevor's eyes caught on a woman walking down the dock behind his friends. He wasn't sure what caught his attention, but she was in no way a wallflower. She oozed confidence with every step. Trevor frowned in curiosity when he took note of what she was wearing.

The thigh-length, bulky tan coat showed off long, well-formed legs to perfection, but her feet were encased in matching mid-calf boots. Trevor glanced up at the sun. Why in the world would anybody wear boots on a gorgeous day like today? And her head. She had something black and shiny attached to her chestnut colored hair. Both appeared to be plastered to her scalp. It glinted and sparkled in the bright sun with every move she made, but he couldn't figure out what it was.

In his peripheral vision, he saw his friends' wave at him. He was thankful his dark glasses kept them from knowing he never in actuality tore his gaze away from the woman behind them while he returned the wave. When the woman looked up to see who the trio greeted, Trevor fought the impulse to duck out of sight. From the safety of those glasses, he met her stare head on and held it.

Silly as it was, Trevor wanted to smirk at the small thrill of victory when she was the first to look away. Convinced he was in control, he stepped away from the rail. He'd check her out in detail when she came aboard. The realization that she could be heading to another berth almost sent him back to the rail to confirm her progress. Trevor forced himself to get a grip and changed course which took him back into the thick of things.

* * * *

Erica knew when she was being watched. She'd had that instinct to some extent ever since she could remember. After joining the firm, she'd worked to hone it until it became yet another reliable asset in her ever growing arsenal. It was because of that instinct that she knew the moment Trevor Cole first laid eyes on her. She hadn't realized it was him until she'd looked up and caught him staring over the railing at her. He couldn't have realized it, but the sun, being generous with its light, not so much its heat, hit him perfectly from her position on the dock. She could see his eyes through the glasses and confirm his stare. Though Erica had seen pictures of the man, she wasn't prepared for the sheer magnetism he exuded. She'd have to be careful she didn't get sucked in. Thank God for his golden blond hair. Blond men were not her type.

Still, she couldn't help but prefer that his first glimpse of her hadn't been when she was wearing a bulky coat and boots. A cool breeze danced across the dock reminding her why she was dressed the way she was. In her brain, she understood her reaction to seeing him for the first time. Over the past day and a half, Erica had immersed herself in everything Trevor Cole. Both the public reports from newspapers and other publications and the private ones that she could only access through Trecam. On a personal level, she liked that he was a decent guy. On a professional one, it sucked.

Because of his boring background, Erica recommended that Caitlyn assign a team. One person on the front lines gathering evidence and protecting Trevor, while the other person ran down the leads. Hoping to avoid the whole audition thing, Erica volunteered for background duty. Her boss took the recommendations under advisement and amended assignment as needed. All except the part where Erica wouldn't have to deal with

Trevor in person. Hence Erica's reluctant appearance on the dock. Caitlyn assigned the lead tracking to Jason.

Not wishing to make her assignment even harder, she decided not to alienate the man before they'd even met. That's why Erica deferentially dropped her gaze first. She turned her attention to the women and the man in the wheelchair in front of her. She knew from her research that the man was Detective Cameron Dobbs and the thin woman was his wife Marcy. Cam and Trevor grew up on neighboring ranches. The two pursued different paths with Trevor going off to college to major in music and Cam heading to the Police Academy, but even distance hadn't cooled their friendship. When Cam was shot in the line of duty a year ago, Trevor bought his current residence in the area and moved closer to help Marcy with Cam's care.

It told Erica a lot about the kind of man Trevor was. He could've hired nurses, but he'd been pretty hands on with Cam's recovery. She didn't want to be, but she couldn't help being impressed with Trevor. At least on paper. Now she was about to meet the man himself. Erica climbed aboard the yacht and joined the party.

Trevor kept his hands planted on the hips of the latest giggling girl who'd cornered him. In part because it was the only way to keep her from plastering herself all over him where he was seated on a stool. But more because he was able to keep her out of his line of sight so he could watch to see if the woman in the coat came to his party. He couldn't help the stab of disappointment that shot through him when she failed to materialize long after Cam, Marcy and their guest boarded. Trevor shook it away. Of course she wasn't coming to his party. She hadn't belonged. Aside from her strange attire, she'd had an expression on her face that indicated a brain was involved. He looked at the current girl chattering away in front of him. That wasn't an issue with this one. Tuning back in, he was annoyed to learn that she was still talking about her nails.

Trevor mustered up his rock star smile. "Sorry, darling. Some friends just arrived that I really must see to." Without waiting for her consent, he set her out of his path and went to find his best friend.

* * * *

Cam fought his way through the crowd to an out of the way corner with Marcy and her friend Winnie. It never ceased to amaze him how many self-absorbed people showed up to these parties. When he'd said, "excuse me," few of them spared him a glance and swayed a millimeter or so out his path. Until they'd felt the cold steel of his chair threatening to take off their legs. He'd even brought his skinny chair. Amazing.

Poor Winnie turned beet red while she stared at a young woman who'd just removed her already skimpy top presumably so the beefcake behind her in the tiny red Speedo which did nothing to conceal a thing could rub sunscreen on her back. Cam knew his wife meant well, but there was no way this Winnie person was a match for Trevor. Marcy had to be the worst matchmaker in history. It brought a smile to his face to remember how she'd been convinced that he was the perfect match for her cousin. Cam'd gone along with it and befriended the cousin to learn how to woo Marcy. Best thing he'd ever done. He'd be the first to cheer when Trevor found the same thing. He glanced at Winnie and fought a grimace. She wasn't it.

Marcy read his expression and flicked his ear. "Give them a chance," she hissed bending close.

"I just don't want to you to be disappointed if the sparks don't fly."

"Don't be ridiculous. Winnie is a lovely woman."

They both looked her way and were dismayed to discover that her reddish tint had become a hideous purple. Marcy stepped in front of the other woman to block her view of whatever shenanigans the young couple was engaging in.

"What am I doing here? How did you talk me into this? What could Trevor see in me when he has all this . . . this . . . this around?" She tugged the collar of her blouse away from her neck. Cam figured the woman was going to pass out if she didn't take a breath soon. He shrugged. That would just get them out of there that much faster.

"Trevor is a great guy. Not at all like these other guys." Marcy looked around. She frowned and Cam turned to follow her gaze. He bit the inside of his cheek to keep from laughing when he saw his friend had a bony blonde hanging on his arm when he made his way toward them. Trevor took one look at Marcy's glower and shook the blonde off to continue the trek alone.

Marcy turned on a smile for Winnie. Patted her hand. The woman looked like she was going to puke at any moment. "Just be your sweet self. None of these women can hold a candle to you. You'll see."

"Hey, guys. I thought you'd never get here." Trevor greeted the trio when he strolled up. He turned on his rock star smile. Cam knew it was for Winnie's benefit. Marcy gave Trevor a big hug and pushed him closer to Winnie.

"Hey, Trev. This is Winnie Winslow. I was bragging about my husband's perfect friend, and she didn't believe you existed so I had to make the introduction." Cam squeezed Marcy's hand. She was trying way too hard. Trevor looked amused.

"Great. I'd like to meet this guy, too." Trevor looked around, and Winnie snorted a giggle. Marcy turned red with embarrassment. Cam yanked her down on his lap and gave Trevor a wolfish grin.

"Now that the two of you have met, would you mind making yourself scarce so I can enjoy my wife for a minute?"

Trevor chuckled. He took Winnie's hand. She looked at him with a serious case of disbelief and hero worship. "I think that's our cue to get lost. You game?"

Star struck, Winnie managed a nod. She looked quite a bit like a bobble head doll, but Trevor retained his smile while he set out to be a good host. He led her away through the crowd.

* * * *

At last, Erica emerged on the main deck of Trevor's yacht. She'd taken advantage of the chaos to explore the boat so the layout in her memory was more detailed than what she'd learned from a blueprint. During her explorations, Erica took the time to appreciate the lushly appointed amenities. Trevor had spared no expense on the dark mahogany which appeared polished within an inch of its life. The heads were done in marble and the furniture thick and comfy. Luxury exemplified.

Now that she'd finished studying the yacht, Erica wanted to get a look at each guest. It was a long shot, but if she could ID his tormentor and put a stop to it at the party, she'd be a very happy camper. And she'd be free for assignment on a juicier case.

She looked over another mindless couple when they raced past her to a stateroom. Erica sighed, a girl could dream.

She made her way up to the Flydeck where she'd glimpsed him heading earlier. Trevor was chatting with the woman who'd arrived with his friends. Erica wasn't sure what surprised her more, that Trevor appeared to be listening or that he'd given his attention to the one female who was still wearing a full set of clothes. Erica considered her own costume hidden under her coat and shrugged. It wasn't quite as revealing as most of what she'd seen, but she didn't want to be lumped in with the rest of the partygoers either. Part of her job today depended on standing out.

She looked around the deck and took a deep breath. It was time. The pool sat in the middle of a casual teak deck crowned with a bubbling hot tub. That many people in one hot tub was just . . . wrong. Erica shook off her shudder and spied a stereo on a shelf at the far side of the deck. She turned her attention back to the pool which was raised about three feet so that meant it couldn't be more than four feet deep like she'd expected.

Routine modifications came to her while she slunk toward the stereo, careful to blend with the crowd. She sat on the ground out of Trevor's view and shed her coat and boots.

The brisk air sent a shiver through her. What kind of nut threw a party on a yacht in this kind of weather? Even packed like it was, the steam rising from the Jacuzzi was pretty inviting. Nothing came from the pool. She shuddered to imagine how cold it was. Surely people would be in it if he kept it heated. Or maybe she was the sole person crazy enough to want to swim in this weather.

Erica slipped the CD in the stereo and pressed play. When the music pounded on the deck, Erica stood up and nailed Trevor with a look. A little thrill of satisfaction shot through her when his head snapped her way. She had his full attention. She saw the crestfallen look on his companion's face, and vowed to feel bad about the interruption later. She did her walk on in time to the music.

Erica hoisted herself up on the side of the pool, holding Trevor's puzzled gaze the entire way. She could feel that other people were watching her little performance, too. Let them watch. She was prepared to be amazing in four feet of water. Trevor would be floored and hire her on the spot. She would put a stop to the threats on his life in record time, and they'd both go their separate ways. All without him being any the wiser, of course.

Trevor hopped up from his seat and raised a hand. Erica smiled at him, confident she had him hooked and slid into the pool. It took just a second for her to realize that there was no water in it. Erica's smile morphed into shock when she saw that the pool was even deeper than she'd figured. The bottom was about seven feet down, and she hit it with a less than graceful thump. The wind whooshed out of her. She landed in a tangled sprawl. She lay there for a moment trying to gather her wits.

* * * *

Trevor hurried to the side of the pool and looked at the woman who'd captured his attention from the dock. What in the world had she been trying to do?

"Are you hurt? Can you move?" he called to her. More guests gathered around the sides of the pool, giggling at her expense.

"Yeah. I think." The last part of her answer was a mere whisper while she experimented with moving each limb. She looked up at the laughing guests and flushed crimson over her entire body. And what a body it was. The woman was a knock out. Long legs attached to full hips. He watched, fascinated, while each muscle flexed during her inventory. She arched her back emphasizing her tempting bosom that barely remained tucked inside the fanciest swimming suit he'd ever seen in his life.

He drew his eyes up to her face and was dismayed to note that she'd caught him checking out her boobs. He fought his own embarrassed flush. "Do you need a hand?"

* * * *

"I've got it," she snapped and climbed to her feet. Erica tried her best to ignore the laughing partygoers and headed for the ladder on the side of the pool. So much for amazing. Her brain scampered for a way to salvage this operation. She reached for a step and was dismayed when the bottom one remained a couple inches higher than her fingertips. Without water, she had no hope of ever reaching it. She looked up at Trevor who was directly over her head with the still dressed woman. Bright side? She'd gotten his attention all right.

Erica swallowed the tattered remains of her pride. Offered him a tiny smile. "Well, maybe I could use a little help."

Trevor grinned at her. "You sure? 'Cause if you've got it?" That grin did things to Erica's insides that she preferred not to think about. She opted to admit just that she understood why he was a star and leave it at that. The man had charisma to spare. She focused on her situation instead.

Erica's own sense of humor returned. Nothing like a former Olympic swimmer trapped in a pool with no water. "I don't got this one."

Trevor laughed when he reached over the side for her. He frowned when he couldn't reach her. "Jump."

Erica shook her head. "And pull you in, too? No way." She propped her hands on her hips while she mused. "My coat's over there. Think you can haul me up with it?"

* * * *

Trevor's brow quirked at the challenge. A little slip of a thing like her? Who was she kidding? Winnie hurried to get the coat before Trevor could move and handed it to him. He hid a grimace when he realized he'd forgotten Winnie was even there. He'd been so delighted to see the woman from the dock at his party.

He let down the end of the coat for her to grab. She wrapped the sleeve around her left arm and looked up at him with a nod. Trevor pulled on the jacket and found that the woman was much heavier than she appeared. While trying to hide it, he gritted his teeth and pulled with all his might. Winnie grabbed the coat too, adding her girth. Little by little, they made progress and the woman was able to gain her footing on the ladder.

Erica hoisted herself over the side. She could see Trevor's surprise that she was just a head shorter than his own six foot three in bare feet. She included both Trevor and Winnie in her grateful smile. "Thanks for the rescue."

She shrugged back into the coat. Inside the pool, she'd been protected from the breeze off the water. Not so on the deck.

"Wanna explain what you were up to?" Trevor looked her over from head to toe. "You don't appear to be drunk. You just have a death wish?"

Erica laughed. She noted how the woman moved possessively to his side. Her intuition told her that would irritate him. The way he stepped away, to turn off his CD that was still blaring from the stereo confirmed her suspicion. Still, not keen to make enemies, and not knowing who the woman was, she addressed her in her answer along with Trevor.

"I was trying to audition."

"Excuse me?" Trevor returned to face her.

"I'm Erica Kellogg." Erica stuck out her hand for a hearty shake from both of them. "I heard that you were looking to diversify your show. I thought what better diversification than to add a synchronized swimmer."

Trevor belted out a laugh. "You? A synchronized swimmer?"

Erica fought to keep her temper in check. "That wasn't one of my better performances."

"What would you synchronize with just one of you? Or should I expect more swimmers to traipse out at any moment?"

Her irritation rising, Erica pasted on a smile to inform him, "You synchronize with the music when there's only one. It's called a solo. And it wouldn't be just me on the stage. I'd be there to enhance your show. You could think of me like an extra stage light."

"I appreciate you for stopping by, but my show is just fine."

He turned away and headed down the stairs to the lower decks. Erica scrambled to grab her boots and follow. The woman looked startled at their abrupt exit and raced to join the procession. She caught up with them on the wheelhouse deck.

"Trevor's right. He doesn't need a swimmer." The woman tried to conceal her labored breathing and stepped between Erica and Trevor.

Trevor looked at the woman in annoyance. It was obvious she'd overstepped her bounds. Erica figured she could use it to her advantage. She addressed the woman.

"You wouldn't have anything to worry about. Our relationship would be strictly professional. Like I said, I'd just be set dressing. Quiet as a mouse."

"But the set is already dressed just fine." Since Trevor was behind her, the woman didn't see his irritated expression. Erica did.

And reveled in it. She might get him to agree to this crazy plan just because someone told him not to do it. That would be fun.

The three of them reached the main deck and threaded their way through the partygoers.

"We all need a change. And this is something no one has seen Trevor do before. Think of the increased ticket sales."

The woman frowned when they joined Cam and Marcy. Marcy gave Erica a curious look that leaned on the unhappy side. "What's going on? Trevor? Winnie?"

Before Trevor could get a word in, the woman said, "This is Erica. She thinks Trevor needs to add a synchronized swimmer to his concerts."

"I heard that he wanted a new flavor. Synchro is definitely a new flavor."

An expression she couldn't read flitted over Cam's face before he turned his attention to Trevor. Erica studied him a little more in detail. Was he the one who'd hired them? The phrase she'd said was the one from the assignment file. It was on the list of arguments Trevor might respond to.

"It might not be a bad idea, Trev. Spice things up a little bit."

Marcy looked at her husband, scandalized. "I don't think now is the right time to change the show." She sided with her friend. "He's about to go on tour. Far too late for such a big change." Marcy looked Erica over. "Do you even know if the woman can swim?"

Erica blushed, and Trevor laughed. "She was about to give us a demonstration, but I emptied the pool this afternoon."

Erica shot him a grateful look that he hadn't rehashed the whole embarrassing episode. Winnie, however, wasn't so kind.

"She fell in. It took the both of us to fish her out."

Trevor didn't look any happier than Erica was at having his faults put on display alongside Erica's.

"You know what? The more I think about it, the more I like it." Trevor leaned against the railing and stroked his chin. Erica got the sense it was more for show than anything else. "You gotta admit. You haven't seen many synchronized swimmers in rock concerts."

Relief flooded Erica. Despite everything that had happened, she was in. "Thank you so much, Mr. Cole! You're not going to regret this."

Winnie and Marcy looked less than thrilled at his decision. Their expressions darkened even further when Trevor pushed off the railing and took Erica's hand. She barely noticed the other women's reactions because she was too busy trying to figure out where that little jolt of electricity had come from. The look on Trevor's face told her he was wondering the same thing.

"Let's go discuss terms."

Erica nodded and let him lead her away.

* * * *

Marcy turned on Cam. "What was that?" she demanded. "Can't you see that little tart just wants Trevor's attention? And things were going so well with him and Winnie."

"Marce, she just wants a job. And if things were going that well with Winnie, he'll be back."

"I can't believe you're taking her side!"

"I'm not taking . . ."

"We need some serious repair work done, here." Marcy's face lit up. Cam eyed her warily.

"Whatever you're thinking, let it go."

"Help me clear the yacht." Marcy popped up off Cam's lap.

"What? I'm not doing that?" Cam folded his arms across his broad chest.

Marcy leveled a glare at him. "Winnie's time was cut short. We're going to set up a nice dinner. For two. Got it?"

"Trev's gonna hate that." Cam reached for Marcy's hand. "Don't you think we've interfered enough for one day?"

Marcy snatched her hand away. "It's not interference if it's for his own good."

"What kind of logic is that?"

Marcy reared up to her full five foot three inches "The kind you'd do well to get behind." She handed him her cell phone. "Luigi's is in my phone book. Make sure they deliver." She grabbed Winnie's hand, and they set off telling everyone that the party was over.

Cam sighed and rubbed his temples. Trevor was going to kill him. He perked up when he remembered Erica. If she was who he believed she was, Winnie was going to be in for a very disappointing night. Cam tried to feel some remorse, but couldn't. Not when she'd turned into a controlling shrew the moment another woman caught Trevor's attention. If they got involved, they'd both go insane before long.

Cam found the number in his wife's phone. Dialed. When it was picked up on the other end, he grinned when he said, "Hi, I'd like to order for three."

Chapter Three

Glad for a moment out of Trevor's sight, Erica lowered her aching body into a nearby chair. She grimaced when her elbow brushed the arm of the chair. Erica paused to listen for any sign of Trevor's return. She could still hear him shuffling papers in his office so she was careful when she shrugged out of one side of her coat. She was dismayed to see bruises beginning to form around her elbow, and her shoulder was tender to the touch. Erica blew out a breath of frustration when she detected some slight swelling. Some bodyguard she was, not double checking to make sure that the pool was filled. Live and learn. She sighed, and pulled the coat back on.

Except in her line of work, the living depended on the learning beforehand. This time, she'd escaped with just a bruise. In the future, she vowed to always confirm the intel gathered from satellite images before leaping into anything. Literally. There was at least one silver lining that came from her folly. There was no way Trevor would ever suspect her true motive for being there. Not the way she'd tumbled into his life. She wiped the amused smile from her face when footsteps signaled his return.

"Standard contract," Trevor remarked with a casual wave of

a sheaf of papers. Never taking his eyes off her, he lowered his tall frame into a chair beside hers. He leaned close so he wouldn't have to yell over the party that was still going strong. Erica fought not to lose herself in his soulful jade eyes. They weren't dead like she'd expected. Far from it. She forced herself to focus on what he was saying.

Trevor regarded her when he leaned back in his seat. "But first, I'd like to hear your vision for the performance."

"My vision?"

"Yeah. Since your audition didn't go as expected, I'd like an idea of what you're thinking. How would you stage it?"

Oh crap. She was in trouble. She didn't know the first thing about staging a show. She spent her day and half of study time learning his life inside and out. Going with her theory that the more inept she looked, there would be less of a chance that he'd deduce her real purpose for being there, Erica decided to bluster her way through. "Well . . . you saw the costume."

"That's it?" Trevor studied her for a long moment. Her instincts screamed that he was sizing her up and found her woefully lacking. "Why are you really here?"

No way could he suspect. Not after her less than graceful performance earlier. Nevertheless, she went with the second version of the truth. "I just want to swim." Erica surprised herself to hear the authenticity resounding in her answer. She thought she'd gotten past missing an audience. It appeared that she'd been wrong. Since the emotion had surfaced, she figured she might as well use it.

* * * *

"There're plenty of pools all over the place. Can't you swim there?" Trevor stared at Erica not quite sure what to make of her. Even though she continued to hold his gaze, he was pretty certain she was looking inward. The silence stretched between them for so long that he was beginning to think she wasn't going to answer him. Until he'd gauged her true intentions, he wasn't giving her that contract. Not with everything that had happened in the past few weeks. And he had every intention of having Cam check her out. Tonight. Make sure she was on the up and up before he allowed her on his payroll.

"It's just not the same without an audience." Her quiet

statement caught him by surprise. "It's . . . indescribable. The feeling you get when you share what you do with others. The energy they exude . . . you feed off of it and it just makes you . . . better." She refocused on him. "That probably doesn't make any sense."

In reality, it made perfect sense. The fact was it was the reason that he still went on tour. He could've retired long ago if that's what he wanted. Every time he got mobbed by crowds of people, the "R" word sprang to mind in an instant. But then he'd go onstage and connect with an audience. The moment that happened, all the other headaches became worth it. He studied Erica. Trying to see if she was putting him on. He didn't expect to see such a pained look in her eyes. She shook it away and smiled.

All reservations flew out of Trevor's head. "Here's what I'm thinking." He slid from the chair to kneel next to the table with a pen and piece of scrap paper. "A glass stage. Fill it with water. You'll swim high above my head." He sketched out his ideas with stick figures. Erica slid to the floor next to him.

"Part of the thrill of synchro is to see what's happening on top of the water."

Trevor nodded and scratched out his drawing. On a clean sheet, he started again. "Okay. So we'll reverse it. I'll be on top of you." Trevor blushed to his hairline when his words registered in his ears. "I mean . . . uh . . ."

Erica's smile put him at ease. "I know what you mean." She studied the rendering. "How wide and long is the tank?"

"What do you need it to be?" Erica shot him a puzzled look. "We'll have to build it," Trevor clarified.

Erica looked like a kid in a candy store who'd just been turned loose with his credit card. "A little movement room, at least nine feet of depth and I'm a happy camper."

Trevor nodded. "The stage runs about twenty five meters . . ." He doodled on the paper. "It should be portable and light."

"Fiberglass is what you want then. Also easier to maintain."

"Maintenance. Hmmm. I wonder if I can convince my pool guy to go on the road. Unless you know one who'll travel with us?"

Erica shrugged. "I know a pool girl, though."

Trevor looked at her and smiled. That was the moment he realized how close they were sitting. All alone. Behind a closed door. He wondered what she'd do if he sampled her full lips with his. The sudden stirring low in his belly served up a warning, and he made haste to revise his train of thought. He'd lose her as a performer for sure. Talking over plans to add her to the show had his creative juices flowing for the first time in quite a while. This thing could work. And it just might be expensive enough to solve his current tax issue. "You're going to be an asset, aren't you?"

* * * *

Erica caught the way his eyes darkened and knew she should move away. He was her client. She was supposed to be protecting him, not leading him on. But her body refused to obey the simple command, and it tuned in to everything around her instead — every puff of air on her heated skin, every smell, especially the subtle cologne he was wearing and something more primal. It strengthened when he leaned closer. But there was another aroma that didn't quite fit. And a sound. Or lack of it.

Just before his lips could meet hers, she tilted her head toward the door to listen. "Do you hear that?"

* * * *

Trevor snapped back to his senses. What was he doing? She was his employee. He couldn't hit on her, much less kiss her. She's not your employee until she signs the contract, an impish little voice reminded him. He shook it away. He wanted her to sign the contract. He put some distance between them. Even though he hadn't gotten to see her swim, his instincts were telling him that she would be amazing. He wasn't about to jeopardize business with a little meaningless pleasure. He could sense her passion for swimming that would demand perfection. That same passion drove his music.

"I don't hear anything." At last, Trevor convinced his mouth to form the words when all it wanted to do was taste her. He tried to shake that idea away.

"That's what I mean. What happened to the party?" With grace, she stood and headed for the door. Now that she'd mentioned it, Trevor noticed that things were indeed much quieter than when they'd snuck away.

* * * *

Erica stepped from the salon and looked around. Her instincts weren't signaling danger, but until she understood why they were alone all of a sudden, she wasn't going to put him at risk. It seemed Trevor had other ideas. He caught up to her and looked around for himself.

"That's odd. Usually I can't get rid of everybody until at least dawn."

Erica sniffed the air. A sudden breeze brought the scent of garlic wafting toward them. Trevor paused, and she watched him inhale. He smiled.

"Luigi's. Mmmm. Polenta Alla Valdostana. Ravioli Rossini, Farfaline al pollo e broccoli. And he always throws in an extra loaf of his fresh baked garlic bread."

Erica looked at Trevor in amazement. "You can smell all that?"

He grinned at her while he slid down to the main deck. "You can't?"

Erica scrambled to catch him. Since he sounded as surprised as she, he couldn't have ordered anything. She knew she hadn't. Where had this food come from? She couldn't shake away a disturbing theory.

She watched Trevor halt in his tracks, and her heart skipped a beat. Had she inadvertently let him run head on into danger? She fingered the switchblade she'd tucked in the back of her costume and rushed to his side.

"Winnie? Where is everybody? What's all this?" Trevor stared at the woman leaning against the rail.

Erica relaxed her grip a bit on the knife when she saw the other woman alone on the deck. A table was set for two complete with candles and flowers.

"I figured you might be hungry." Her smile faded when she noticed Erica just over his shoulder. "And you're still here."

Erica opened her mouth to reply, but Trevor beat her to it. "It's awfully nice of you to feed us like this. I'm afraid we got a little caught up in work, and the time just flew by."

Erica admired the way he misunderstood Winnie's intentions. Winnie opened her mouth to correct him, but seemed to reconsider. Her smile was a little more brittle this time around.

"I just wanted to help."

"You have." He inspected the table. "How'd you know to get all my favorites?"

Erica tensed at the question. How, indeed?

Winnie giggled. "I might've had a little help from Cam. He's a great guy."

Erica heard the ring of truth in the other woman's statement and relaxed her grip on the switchblade.

"Good man." Before Winnie could protest, Trevor swept a third chair over to the table for Erica and seated both women before taking a seat himself. It was interesting to Erica that he'd seated her between them and didn't appear to have even considered asking her to leave. Erica was relieved. She had no intention of leaving him alone until he was safely tucked in his bed back at the mansion. She didn't care if it were alone or not. The yacht was too much of an open target for her to leave him there. If he'd decided to stay, she would have to come up with a plausible story to remain, too, but she'd cross that bridge when she got to it.

* * * *

Trevor kept up a running commentary while he served up all three dishes to each of them. The fact that there were three dishes let him know that Cam expected Erica to stay. He'd also figured that Marcy was the one behind the abbreviated party. He had to give the woman credit for being determined, even if her matchmaking skills left a whole lot to be desired. He smiled at Erica while she tried everything he put on her plate with gusto. Winnie pretended to eat. She did manage a few bites and he could tell she enjoyed those, but she just wouldn't eat any more. Another strike against her.

"Mmmm," Erica sighed and sat back in her chair after cleaning her plate. "That was delicious. I can't believe I've never tried this restaurant before."

"See why it's my favorite?" His smile included Winnie in the conversation. "What'd you think?"

She gave a polite nod at the food still on her plate. "It was very good. I'm just sorry I couldn't eat more." She looked at Erica. "You sure did some damage though. Aren't you afraid of losing that lovely figure?"

Trevor eyed Erica when she looked at the woman. Her dig came through loud and clear judging by Erica's tight smile. It seemed she felt the same way about Winnie that he did. Less of the woman was definitely more. What on earth was Marcy thinking?

"I swim at least three miles a day. And I'm thankful to have a high metabolism." She smiled, radiating innocence. Trevor refused to admit he enjoyed the sour look that flitted over Winnie's plump face. "My only worry tends toward whether there's dessert or not. Speaking of . . ." Erica turned to him.

Trevor retrieved another bag and pulled out an aromatic concoction of chocolate. Erica inhaled in appreciation. He smiled while he served up the dish to all three of them. Winnie indicated that she just wanted a small piece and Trevor was happy to oblige. More for him and Erica.

"Ah, if only I had the time for that luxury. How do you find the time to work?"

"Actually, I'm down to a fifteen minute mile in open water and a little faster in a pool. It really doesn't take too long." Erica smiled at Trevor. The woman just got better and better. Now he was listening with an employer's ear more than his I'm-on-a-bad-date-save-me ear. "And now that swimming is my job, I expect to train even longer."

Trevor returned the smile and watched in satisfaction while Erica savored every bite. He was irritated when Winnie just took a small bite or two then pushed the dessert away. Having come from a family who'd not been wealthy, Trevor appreciated the cost of things. By his calculation, Winnie wasted about forty dollars' worth of food that evening. Now that he'd come into some success, he was vigilant about being wasteful. His band even joked at his expense when he took his leftovers home from the restaurants they'd frequent while on the road. He'd always have the last laugh when the midnight munchies hit and he was the one who had a snack on hand.

Trevor polished off the last of his dessert and stretched. "Such a lovely meal shared with two beautiful ladies. Thank you, both. But I'm afraid I need to call it a night." He gave them a sheepish smile. "Not as young as I used to be."

"Of course." Erica got up and began clearing the table. She

looked at Winnie. "Did you want to take any of this with you?"

Winnie looked appalled at the question. She risked a glance at Trevor then turned her nose up at Erica. "I'm finished. Thank you."

Erica shrugged and dumped the woman's plate into an empty bag. Winnie stood and pulled Trevor to his feet and smiled up at him.

"Everything was wonderful. Did you enjoy the break?"

From the corner of his eye, he watched Erica put the leftovers still in their containers aside and stack the china. Trevor tried to remember the question. "Yes. Do you need a cab, or did you drive?"

Erica's lips quirked like she was fighting a smile when Winnie blustered, "I . . . I . . . uh rode with the Dobbs."

Trevor nodded and checked his watch. "We'll call you a cab from here. I'll walk you up to the restaurant on the dock to wait after I close things up. Sound good?"

Winnie's expression left no doubt that she hated the idea. Surely she hadn't imagined he would take her home with him. Erica on the other hand . . . The woman recovered and smiled.

"That sounds perfect." She eyed Erica, hoping she would be the first to leave. "What about you? Share a cab?" Winnie offered, sugar dripping from every syllable.

"I drove. But I appreciate the gesture." Erica picked up their dishes. "It won't take me a moment to wash these."

Trevor put up a hand stopping her. "There's a dishwasher. I'll load it when I do my walk through." Erica nodded and handed the dishes to him. It was obvious she was looking for something to do. Winnie grabbed the bag of leftovers.

"I'll just throw these out."

"No!" Trevor and Erica protested together. They looked at each other in surprise. Trevor nodded in deference to Erica, curious to see what she was thinking.

"It'd be a shame to waste that much food. I'll take it." She shot a questioning look at Trevor. "Unless you . . ."

"It's all yours." Trevor watched Winnie hand the food over to Erica. Seemed like he wouldn't be the only one taking a doggy bag with him while on the road. His smile was hidden when he hurried off to secure the yacht.

* * * *

Erica kept a vigilant eye on Trevor when he was in the open on the upper decks. She looked around the darkened marina trying to ascertain any threat that might be awaiting them.

"Trevor is a nice guy," Winnie remarked while they stood ready to disembark.

"He is, isn't he? I think I'm going to like working for him."

"Cut the crap. We both know you're not here to work for him." Winnie glared at Erica. "But you've certainly put on quite the performance today."

"Excuse me?" Erica was surprised at the venom spewing from the woman's mouth all of a sudden.

"Miss I Swim Three Miles A Day. I bet you don't even know how to swim."

"I didn't come here to crash your date or whatever it is you have going," Erica tried to explain.

"The two of us were having a perfectly lovely time before you pulled your little stunt. And don't think Marcy isn't onto you, too."

"That's a good trick. Since there's nothing to be onto."

"All set, ladies?" Trevor joined them. Judging by his expression, Erica could tell that he'd heard quite a bit of the exchange.

Winnie turned on a winsome smile. "Ready when you are." She stepped closer and tried to link her arm with his, shutting Erica out.

Trevor stepped out of reach. "I think I might've given you the wrong impression."

Winnie frowned up at him. Erica melted back into the shadows in an attempt to be less intrusive. Still, she stayed near enough in case things turned unpleasant. She was his bodyguard. The job didn't end with just people who wanted him dead previous to her assignment.

"I don't know what you're talking about."

"I'm really sorry Marcy got you thinking the two of us could become a couple. It's not gonna happen."

Winnie reared up in anger and embarrassment. Erica eased from her position in case she needed to take the woman down.

From her spot behind Trevor, Erica narrowed her eyes to dangerous slits and stared hard at Winnie. Daring her to make a move.

Winnie's eyes widened telling Erica she'd gotten her point across. Instead, the woman tossed her hair over her shoulder with what looked to Erica to be a very haughty look.

"Your loss." Winnie spun on her heel and stalked her way off the yacht. Erica dropped her aggressive posture when Trevor turned to face her.

"I think we should give her a minute." He leaned against a wall and watched Winnie stomp her way up the dock. Erica kept her vigil also.

"You did the right thing."

"I hate when that happens." Trevor ran a hand over his face. "Women get it in their heads I'm theirs because I show them a little respect and next thing you know, they have us married with eight kids on a farm."

A smile quirked on Erica's lips. He looked at her.

"I'm just telling you this as a warning. If you're going with us on tour, you'll see a lot more of this. I don't want you to be uncomfortable or think I'm a jerk."

"Because there's no way you could actually be a jerk, you mean," Erica teased.

He turned a surprised look on her. Smiled. "I have my moments."

Erica turned her attention to Winnie's retreating back. "So why don't you have your bodyguard handle these little confrontations?" She'd been dying to probe his reasons for refusing protection all day. At last, she was able to half seize, half create the opportunity.

"A man doesn't hand these things off to someone else." So much for her probing investigation. "Besides, I'm kinda in between bodyguards at the moment."

Erica wanted to smile at that. As far as he knew anyway. The smile was forgotten when she noticed that the yacht appeared to be drifting away from the dock. "Are we moving?"

"What?" Trevor rushed to the rail. The gangplank pulled loose and dropped into the water with a splash. Erica joined him. "I think the anchor came loose."

He turned and sprinted up to the wheelhouse deck. Erica

was hot on his heels. The controls were still off, but there was no question that they were moving. Faster than a mere drift. Erica reached to turn on the controls, but a sudden surge of speed caught them both by surprise. Trevor and Erica tumbled backward and landed in a heap just outside the wheelhouse.

"Are you okay," Trevor asked. Erica bolted to her feet and headed back inside. Clueless about what to do, Erica searched for a way to stop the yacht.

"Do you know how to control this thing?" She looked at Trevor when he joined her in the search.

"I have a captain who takes us out on occasion. He showed me the basics. They went over my head."

Erica nodded while she picked up the phone on the console. She listened a moment, hit the switch hook then shook her head. "Dead."

"Something has to work." Trevor gestured out the window when the scenery began to fly by faster and faster. Other vessels scrambled to get out of their way. Some of their captains honked. Others just made rude gestures.

"C'mon." Erica grabbed his hand and led him back to the main deck. She strapped them both in life jackets then headed for the rail. Trevor grabbed her arm.

"What are you doing? We're not jumping in that."

"We have to get off the yacht."

"Now's not the time to panic," Trevor said, his tone reassuring. Erica almost laughed. Her instincts were screaming that they were in for a worse fate if they didn't jump, but she was far from panicked. At the speed they were traveling, they would be too far from shore and out of options in a very short amount of time.

"Maybe we can shut her down at the engine." Trevor stared at the water. She could almost see the trepidation rolling off him in waves. Erica knew she was going to have to do some coaching to get him in there.

Erica watched the shore disappear while they lurched farther out to sea. Against her better judgment, she nodded her agreement. Maybe his idea would work. She and Trevor raced below the deck to the engine room.

"What the . . ." Trevor said when he stopped short. Erica wanted to finish the sentiment when she heard that the engines were silent. "They're not even on. How is this happening?"

Erica took his hand in hers and gave it a pat. "I don't know. But something is propelling us . . ." Erica headed back to the main deck where she did a slow walk around the yacht's perimeter. Trevor followed and watched her work. She noted the suspicious look in his eye, but she'd have to deal with that later.

Erica almost walked by it. She backed up and stared at the expanse of water before them. She could just make out a larger vessel cutting through the water directly ahead. She frowned and looked at the otherwise empty sea. Erica leaned on the rail to stare at the water below.

"What's wrong?" Trevor joined her at the rail. She sucked in a breath of surprise.

"Crap." She pointed out some kind of line that was attached to the yacht. The vessel was towing them. The line splashed when the vessel made a sharp turn.

"I don't know. Something attached to the hull." She leaned out for another look. "I think I might be able to reach it. Cut us loose."

Trevor shook his head. "I don't think we have time."

"This isn't the moment to be Mr. Negative."

"How about Mr. Realistic?" Trevor placed his hands on either side of Erica's head and turned it. She gasped when she saw they were speeding toward a jagged rock cliff.

Chapter Four

Erica grabbed Trevor by his life jacket and demanded, "How much fuel is onboard?"

"I dunno. Full tank usually."

Erica blew out a breath of frustration. And of course they weren't using any of it being pulled the way they were. "Get to the back rail."

Trevor shook his head. "I know you aren't thinking of jumping now. The water has to be freezing. And the marine life. I'm sure some are poisonous."

"So you'd rather burn to death than take your chances in a little cold water." Erica dragged him toward the back.

"It's a whole lot more than a little." Trevor pushed her away. "You go. Make sure the authorities know what happened out here."

"We both go or we both stay. Your call."

Trevor shook his head. "I'm so sorry you were dragged into this."

Erica checked the rapidly approaching rock face. They were going to smash into it starboard. The other vessel sped up and disappeared into the night. "You mean you know who's behind this?"

"No. I just . . ."

"We don't have time for this." Erica unfastened his life jacket and crisscrossed the straps with hers. She stared in his frightened eyes. The set of his jaw told her he'd never admit his fear. "We're gonna be fine."

"No!" He tried to unfasten the straps. "I can't swim."

Erica smacked his hands away. "I know."

"I'll just take you down with me."

Erica smiled and held his hands. "Jump!"

She did the jumping, while he flopped over the side. Hooked together, they splashed in the yacht's wake and were sucked under.

Erica felt, more than saw Trevor's chest begin to heave. His hands worked at unfastening the jacket again. Erica pressed close to him, so his fingers would have no room to work. She caught his face in her hands to steady him. Made him focus on her. His frantic movements calmed, and they reached neutral buoyancy.

Lungs beginning to burn, Erica blew out the air in a steady stream. She righted them and followed the bubbles to the surface. Trevor followed her lead and flutter kicked for all he was worth. Erica caught his attention again and shook her head. She guided his legs into rhythm with hers as they rose.

The moment their heads broke the surface, Trevor and Erica both sucked in some much needed oxygen. They huddled there, just breathing for a long moment. With a loud crunch, the yacht slammed into the rock face. The explosion lit the night sky and sent bits, pieces and chunks into the air. Erica tried to estimate where the debris would land so she could guide Trevor out of harm's way. The task proved futile when pieces of the yacht seemed to pelt them from all sides. They only had one option left.

"We gotta go under!"

Trevor shook his head. "No."

Erica didn't bother with a rebuttal. She jumped and sunk under the water pulling him with her just when a chair splashed down overhead. Trevor looked up and shuddered. Erica tugged him away. Gasping for air, the two surfaced just out of range of the still landing objects. Trevor looked between the burning yacht and Erica. She gave him a reassuring smile.

"I'm going to swim us to shore. Ready?"

Trevor looked at the cliff where the yacht crashed and shook his head. "That's too far. Can't we just float here?"

Erica smiled. "So now you want to take your chances with the poisonous sea creatures?"

"No, I just can't . . ."

"You wanted to know if I could swim, right?" Trevor gave her a brief nod and hung onto her. Erica maneuvered them into position and side kicked toward the shore. She had just enough light from the fire to navigate.

It took a moment to get her rhythm. She was used to the synchro side kick where the top leg went forward. In the rescue side kick it went backward. Hauling Trevor like she was, it didn't take her long to figure out why. She couldn't grab enough water the synchro way to propel them effectively.

"Up, out, together," Erica chanted while she tried to get in the groove. She hated that her boots more or less slid through the water instead of giving her the catch she needed, but she wasn't about to ditch them. Not if they were headed to the tiny island she'd guessed they were near.

"What are you saying?" Trevor asked.

"I'm talking my legs through the kick. Up. Out. Together." She demonstrated the kick move by move. "It's opposite of what I'm used to. But I think I've got it now." She looked him over the best she could in the close proximity and the fading light. "How're you doing?"

"Feeling a little silly letting you do all the work."

"We'll be in the surf in a bit. Then we'll let the water do all the work." She felt him tense.

"In the surf?"

"Yeah. You know how the waves break at the shore?" They rose up on a large wave. "Here we go."

Trevor clung to her while they body surfed the wave. She could feel his whole body trembling. Erica frowned when his fingers dug into her back even through her thick coat. After what seemed to be forever, but was just a few seconds, they were back on the surface. Trevor sputtered and coughed.

"You okay?"

He gave her a jerky nod. Then changed his mind. "I guess now's not the time to tell you about the time my brother and I almost drowned."

Erica frowned. She hadn't come across that little tidbit in her research. "We're almost to the shore. Think you can make it a little longer?"

"The waves are so big." Trevor squeezed his eyes closed and held his breath while they rode a second wave.

"Not yet. You have to breathe right now." Erica rubbed his head and kept an eye on the water. "Blow it out."

Trevor obeyed.

"Good. Now, wait. Wait . . . Big breath and hold." They sucked in air when they crashed over the wave and went under.

* * * *

Erica put her face close to Trevor's and blew out a bubble. It took him a minute to understand, but he followed her lead and exhaled bubble by bubble like she was doing. The tightness in his lungs eased with each puff. Before he knew it, they were on the surface again. She was smiling at him like he was the greatest thing since sliced bread. She must have some imagination as cowardly as he was behaving. His grip on her was so tight that he'd ceased to have sensation in his fingers several minutes ago. He was too embarrassed to consider what she must think of him so he tried to make his mind go blank instead. Bad plan. All he could see then were the waves crashing over him and Jordan when he was three and Jordan five.

"Trevor? Stay with me. You're doing great."

Erica's voice cut through the painful memories. He clung to her words like he did her body—both, his lifeline. He could see another wave forming over her shoulder and stared at that instead. She caressed his cheeks and shook her head.

"No. Look at me. Focus on me." Trevor tore his eyes away from the wave that seemed to tower over them. Erica glanced over her shoulder.

"We're going under."

"That thing'll crush us."

"That's why we're going under. Ready?"

Trevor found enough strength to nod. She'd gotten them this far.

"Deep breath."

They both sucked in air and went beneath the surface just when the wave crashed above them. Trevor was surprised when his shoulder scraped the bottom. A little of his breath escaped, but he held onto the rest. He'd never been so glad to see land—feel really—in his life. But Erica was tugging him upward. He shook his head. Now that he'd found land, he was sticking to it.

Erica shifted so she had her feet on the ground. Still attached to him, she shoved off and shot them both back to the surface. Trevor sputtered and coughed while he fought for air.

"What'd you do that for? Land is a good thing."

"The currents on the bottom will take us back out to sea. We have to stay on top of them."

Trevor's hopeful expression melted away. She squeezed the base of his neck.

"Hey. We're almost there. The bottom that close is a good sign."

Trevor nodded.

She looked behind them, gauging the waves. "Deep breath."

They rode the wave closer to the shore. All of a sudden, Trevor's feet hit the ground and his head above water. He looked at Erica in amazement. Before he could praise her, she grabbed his hand and headed for dry land. He was surprised to see that she'd unfastened their lifejackets so they were no longer attached. Trevor picked up his knees and splashed his way to safety.

Once beyond the surf, Erica sprawled on the rocky beach with a sigh. She gave him a smile. "You did it."

"You did it. Thank you." Trevor sank down beside her. "That was . . . I never want to do that again."

"C'mon. Admit it. You had fun." Erica tried to hold onto her smile, but her chattering teeth got the better of her. She looked at Trevor and noticed him shivering, too.

"I'm sure fun was had. Just not by us." Trevor rubbed his arms for warmth. Erica pushed herself up.

"We've gotta find some shelter and get a fire going."

"Let's stay near the yacht. Surely someone's gotta see that fire. We'll be rescued in no time."

"We'll freeze long before that happens." Erica pushed to her feet. Tried to pull Trevor up, too. He wouldn't budge.

"So we build a fire here."

"It's too open. It'll be hard to keep a fire going. Besides, if we're where I think we are, there are some caves nearby."

Trevor sprang to his feet. "You know where we are? Is this place populated?"

"First order of business is shelter. Then fire. Come on." Erica trekked off along the rocky beach leaving Trevor no choice but to follow.

* * * *

The longer they walked, the more Erica doubted her memory. She'd come to this island during her first assignment with the Trecam Group. The mistress of a prominent CEO had been mistaken for his wife and kidnapped. The guy responsible delighted in puzzles and led them on a treasure hunt. He'd hidden one clue in a cave on this tiny island. If indeed this was the same island. They'd been clustered together in the ocean.

Erica turned to check Trevor's progress. He was pretty fit for one she assumed was a pampered rock star. He didn't have any gym memberships, but that didn't mean he didn't have a gym at home or work out in hotel fitness centers while on the road. She smiled when she noticed that he stayed right beside her. Always walking on the outside to be positioned between her and danger. In this case, the outside was the ocean. He couldn't realize the thick vegetation on the other side was far more treacherous. His attempt at chivalry made her smile. She'd noticed several little things along those lines that he did without even seeming to think about them.

* * * *

Trevor was dying. He couldn't believe the fast pace Erica was keeping. Still, he was determined to keep up with her. He couldn't let her sole opinion of him be based on that cowardly meltdown he'd had in the water. He shook off those memories. Turning his thoughts instead to their predicament.

He'd never imagined that he'd ever be shipwrecked on a deserted island. Was it in fact deserted, though? What if some forgotten tribe had taken up residence? He was positive that they wouldn't like strangers popping in unannounced. And what if there were a volcano? The tribesmen wouldn't hesitate to sacrifice a tender morsel like Erica to their volcano deity no matter what he did to protect her.

Trevor skidded to a halt. Both mind and body. What in the world was he thinking? He must be delusional if he figured that was how this thing was going to play out. There weren't any rogue tribes waiting for their chance to capture their hapless visitors. See, he scolded himself, this is what happens when you give fear an inch. One minute you're hiring a bodyguard, the next you're seeing homicidal pygmies where there are none. No thanks!

"Trevor?" Erica put a hand on his arm, startling him out of his musings. "You okay?"

Trevor pulled away from her touch, working hard to keep his rock star smile on his face. "Great. I'm great."

She studied him for a long moment. It was like she knew what he'd been thinking. He prayed he hadn't been that transparent. Trevor held her stare. Finally, she let up and tucked the offending hand in her coat pocket.

"I know you're tired. It shouldn't be much farther."

Trevor fought to hold on to his smile and nodded. The moment she turned away, he grimaced. He was delusional. Had to be. No other explanation was logical. Trevor decided to reflect on his unwitting companion. Though he was sorry she'd gotten caught up in this with him, he wasn't sorry to have company. Especially company who looked like her. He considered their short acquaintance and found he was impressed with her on more levels than her beauty. The woman had brains and guts to spare. Focused on his recent panic in the water, he was very much lacking the latter. He was glad she was around. She turned to give him a questioning look. Even though he knew the view to be better with her in it, he hurried to catch up.

* * * *

Erica slowed the pace a fraction. She didn't want Trevor to pass out on her. Something had to be wrong the way he'd started to lag behind. The moment they found shelter and got a fire going, she was going to check him from head to toe for injuries.

Erica squinted into the darkness. It could just be her, but she thought she could make out a section in the rock face that was a bit darker than the rest. Had she found the caves? Not wanting to get Trevor's hopes up, she fought the urge to run ahead and cheer and shout. They were on it soon enough anyway.

A relieved smile lit Erica's face when she discovered that it was indeed one of the caves she'd remembered.

Trevor stared at her for a moment. Asked, "What is it?"

"Our accommodations for the night." She pulled a cigar lighter from her pocket and flicked open the flame. "Maybe. I'll check it out."

She moved toward the entrance, but he grabbed her arm, stopping her.

"That's too dangerous. I should check it out."

Erica gave him an amused look. "Why?"

"Well, because, I'm the man. That's what we do."

Erica just about stifled her giggle. "Well, The Man. Do you have a light?"

"You do."

"And that's why I get to check it out." She tried to pull out of his grasp, but he held on.

"No way. It's too dangerous."

"That's why I'm going first. A whole lot more people would miss you than would miss me." She squirmed out of his grasp and went inside the cave.

* * * *

Trevor stared after her. He replayed their entire association in his mind. When he removed his gratification toward her from the equation, suspicions that had just begun to creep around his brain suddenly solidified in his consciousness. He wasn't in the least bit happy with what he'd figured out. The pygmies were only a pace or so behind.

The competence he'd admired in her had to be a given in light of what he now suspected. It was no wonder she'd been so efficient in getting them off the yacht and to land without the least little indicator of panic. Now that he was thinking it over, there was no way it was a coincidence that she'd been on his yacht today for the party. Yeah, she said she wanted a job, but the timing was far too pat.

As was her handling of him. It had been short work for her to get him to agree to hire her for the show. Before she'd even proven she could swim no less. He had to admit, the idea of a synchronized swimmer in a rock show was a novel concept. He did like being different. Maybe he should go ahead with the idea, but with a different swimmer.

The moment the notion crossed his mind, his gut seized. He knew in his gut that Erica's feelings would be hurt if he went forward without her. No matter how good she was at manipulating him, she hadn't been faking her love for swimming. No. That sentiment had come from deep inside her, and it spoke to something deep inside him.

Erica came out of the cave, and Trevor forced a smile to his lips. Her sure footsteps reminded him of why he was upset with her. Maybe they could still do the show. If only he could get her to drop the other nonsense.

"It's a little cramped, but no other critters seemed to have claimed this cave for their home. We can build a fire near the mouth and stay pretty warm for the night."

He raised an eyebrow and stared at her. "That your professional opinion?"

"What?"

"What's next, chief?"

* * * *

Erica studied Trevor. She couldn't imagine what had happened in the thirty seconds it'd taken her to secure the cave, but something must have. They didn't have time to pursue it now. They had to get a fire going.

"Wood." She looked around the rock face and into the trees. "We should be able to gather what we need."

Trevor followed Erica and helped get the wood. His body language screamed that he was ticked about something. Erica didn't have the slightest clue what. A few minutes later, they were tucked inside the cave sitting near a roaring fire to dry them out.

Erica pulled off her boots and wiggled her numb toes near the heat. She looked at Trevor who in his obstinacy kept everything on and tried to turn his body like a rotisserie chicken. It didn't work very well because the cave was too short for either of them to stand to their full height. He settled for rolling on the cold ground.

"You should take off your shoes and socks at least. They'll dry faster that way," Erica suggested. She shrugged out of her coat and spread it next to the warmth. Even though it didn't offer much coverage, Erica was grateful for her suit since it was already dry.

"I'm fine, thank you."

Erica frowned at his stilted tone. Gone was the camaraderie they'd shared earlier. She didn't understand it. And she wasn't about to put up with a temper tantrum.

"You wanna get whatever it is off your chest now?"

Trevor stared at her for a long moment. "I changed my mind. I don't think you'll be joining my show after all."

Erica raised an eyebrow. She couldn't imagine what she'd done to change his mind. Other than save his life.

"What? Why?" She injected a little hurt in her voice. "I had my heart set on swimming again."

"Cut the crap, Erica. If that's even your name." He stood to pace, his frustration rolled off him in waves, but his bent posture prevented it from being effective so he sat down again. "I know you're my bodyguard."

Chapter Five

"What I don't know is who hired you." Trevor stared at her, a hard, betrayed look on his face.

How in the world had he figured that out? Erica worked to keep a confused expression on her face. "Are you nuts? Do I really look like some big, beefy bodyguard?"

Trevor barked a mirthless laugh. "That's the genius of it. They send you in with your hot little figure and synchronized swimming thinking I'd never be the wiser. Well, I got your wiser right here." Trevor spun on the floor until his back was to her, shutting her out.

Erica opened her mouth to protest, but she gasped instead when the mother of all cramps set in her leg. She rubbed at it frantically, but the muscle refused to relax. She wasn't surprised. Cold water always had that effect on her. It was the intensity that knocked her for a loop.

Erica gritted her teeth and leaned against the cave wall. She would not cry. Especially now. Trevor would think she was faking. She had to find a way to get back in his good graces. But she'd have to figure out how after the cramp went away.

* * * *

Satisfied that he had her where he wanted her, Trevor threw a smirk over his shoulder at Erica. He was surprised to see her gripping her leg and sucking in short gasps of air. Forgetting his anger, he crawled over to her.

"Erica? What is it? What's wrong?" He put a hand on her cheek trying to get her to look at him, but she kept her eyes screwed shut while clutching at her calf. "Talk to me, Erica. What's wrong with your leg?"

For a moment, Trevor suspected she was playing him. Then he touched her leg and was shocked that the muscle was hard like the rock floor they were sitting on. He replaced her hands with his and massaged for all he was worth. Teeth clamped, she sat back and let him.

The cramp was a stubborn bugger. It moved from muscle to muscle. The moment he'd gotten one worked out, another would clench. Trevor would fight that one, too.

He could see in her face that the pain was excruciating, but she never made a sound. Not one tear fell. They pooled beneath her lids, but they didn't make it down her cheeks. Like she'd done for him in the water, he talked her through it.

"Just relax, hon. Feel how it eases with every second that passes." He kneaded and kneaded until his forearms threatened to revolt. "Doesn't that feel better? The pain is going away. See how the muscle is relaxing. Just keep breathing."

It took a while, but Trevor could feel the muscle settle into a more natural state. He eased up on the pressure, but remained vigilant for any others that might be locking down.

"Thank you," Erica said when she could breathe again. The man had amazing hands.

"You're welcome," Trevor breathed. The woman had great legs.

* * * *

Erica couldn't tell if he was trying to prevent the cramp from returning or if he just wanted an excuse to keep touching her. Since it felt so good, she wasn't about to protest. He continued the massage while he asked, "What was that?"

Erica shook her head trying to blow it off. Some kind of bodyguard she was turning out to be. The light bulb flicked on in her head. Maybe she could use this . . .

"The cold water. Makes my legs cramp." She experimented with flexing the offending leg. "Though it's never been that bad."

Trevor kept up the massage. Subtly, his hands changed their objective and began caressing her calf instead. For a moment, she sat mesmerized at the warmth spreading through her. It had nothing to do with the fire flickering beside her. Erica met Trevor's eyes head on. She saw that a little of that warmth was heating him, too.

Trevor broke the silence, but not the contact. "Good to know. We'll make sure the water in your tank is heated."

His words could have a couple meanings. However, she needed them back on track. "You mean I'm not fired. You're dropping this bodyguard nonsense? I mean, what kind of a bodyguard is a near cripple?"

"Consider it dropped. For now." Trevor regarded her. "Though I should probably fire you anyway."

"You can't be blaming me for what happened on your yacht." She slanted him a look. "Will I need to hire a bodyguard to hang around you? It seems like you attract danger." She watched his expression turn thoughtful. He continued to rub her leg. Erica knew she should move, but wasn't in a hurry to break their connection. Besides, she didn't want to jar him out of his thoughts. She'd been dying to broach the subject with him all day. She needed to hear his take on what was going on.

"You might." He smiled his rock star smile for her. He wasn't going to say anymore. Erica pulled her leg from his grasp and sat up to look him square in the eye.

"I'm serious, Trevor. After I read about that bomb, I almost decided not to audition for you. And now your yacht . . ." She threw a vague gesture toward the cave opening. "What is going on?"

"Honestly? I don't know. Idle threats come with the territory. Bombs and yachts towed into cliffs are foreign to me." He sat beside her, draping his arms over his knees. "You shouldn't worry though. Once we go on tour we'll be perfectly safe. The cops will arrest the culprit long before we get back."

Erica heard truth in his statement and studied Trevor. He even looked content to leave it to the cops. It wasn't that he was trying to be difficult and not hire a bodyguard. It seemed to her that he didn't believe he was worthy of one. That and something she couldn't quite put a finger on. She was baffled about how to deal with this assignment. Spoiled, arrogant brats she could handle. Humble, down to earth celebrities she wasn't so sure. She hadn't even known they existed until just now.

"We should get some sleep. I think morning's gonna be here before we know it." Erica lay by the fire and draped her coat over her. She held up the edge for Trevor to join her. He shook his head.

"I'm fine. I'll . . ."

"It's gonna get cold. We need to share the warmth."

* * * *

Trevor looked at Erica holding up her coat in invitation. How he wished it were a different invitation. The fact alone made it impossible for him to join her. He'd already overstepped the boundaries by massaging her leg long after it had ceased needing the massage.

She sat up and smirked at him. "Don't tell me you're a prude."

"Come on, now. I'm a Rock Star, baby. I couldn't be a prude if I wanted to." Trevor injected all the swagger he could find into his voice. He watched Erica try to bite back a giggle. It was clear she didn't believe him. He wasn't sure if he should be offended or just hurt. "I'm just watching out for your virtue. That's all."

This time she did laugh. "Very sweet of you. Now, would you get in? I'm freezing."

Trevor met her challenging look with one of his own. She'd asked for it. He couldn't be responsible for his actions being snuggled up with temptation like that. Who was he kidding? His parents raised him to be a gentleman first. Darnn them.

He scooted next to her then tucked the coat around them both, and then prepared for a restless, tortuous night. Remembering her blush earlier, he decided to share the misery. Trevor molded himself to her and draped a leg over hers. She stiffened. Smirking behind her back, he said, "You were right. This is much warmer."

"Much," Erica agreed. "Now would be a good time." Erica said her body relaxing bit by bit.

He rested his chin on the top of her head. "A good time for

what?" He couldn't believe how good she smelled even after their unexpected swim. And don't get him started on how well she fit against him. It took every bit of his self-control to keep his hand from splaying across her flat stomach and imagining how it would feel expanding with his child . . . What the heck had just crossed his mind? A kid? He wasn't ready for a kid—and with Erica no less. He'd just met the woman. He remembered how she'd tumbled into the pool, and a grin pulled at his lips. Maybe there was such a thing as love at first sight. Whoa! Trevor had to get a grip. What was it about this woman that had him thinking of hearth and home? If he were smart, he'd get up right now and take his chances with the freezing to death. It was quite obvious that he was pretty dumb because he stayed right where he was.

"Were you very young when you almost drowned?"

Her quiet question was even more effective than the cold shower he now longed for. Who did she think she was asking such personal questions? They'd just met! He wanted to tell her to take a hike. Then he realized that in his snuggling, his hand had decided—of its own volition—to get comfortable by cupping a healthy portion of her breast. Who was he to claim a personal violation when he'd been the first offender?

"I was three. Jordan was five." Because he'd been so young at the time, it was hard for him to remember the incident. His subconscious mind, on the hand, was very quick to sound warnings whenever he got too close to being submerged in that much water again. Much like he'd been tonight.

"Do you remember much about it?"

Erica's voice brought him back to the present. He appreciated that she hadn't once mentioned his almost drowning them in his fear. He shook his head and moved his hand to her shoulder like he'd meant to all along.

"The water was really white and choppy. I see Jordan reaching for me. But that's about it."

He felt Erica inhale for another question, but she held it for a minute as if deciding whether or not to ask. Like he'd known she would, she went for it.

"And Jordan?"

Now Trevor understood her hesitation. "He's a salvage diver with the Navy." Trevor shrugged. "He's always been much better at facing down his fears than I am. Probably 'cause he's the firstborn."

* * * *

Erica smiled at the affection she heard in his voice when the subject turned to his family. From her research, she'd known Trevor was one of five, but she hadn't had time to dig very much deeper. She justified this interrogation as background research instead of classifying it as her simply being interested. He was a client and nothing more. It didn't matter that her body wanted his hand to return from her shoulder to its previous resting place. To keep it from looking like she knew too much, Erica asked, "It's just the two of you?"

"Five. Jordan, Sarah, me, Lucy, and Adam."

"And you're in the middle of all that!" Erica shifted on the hard rock floor. "No wonder you're so levelheaded."

Trevor chuckled. "I like to think it's just maturity. Lord knows, I was a handful when I was little. My mom still prays every day that I have a kid just like me so I can see what I put her and Dad through."

"And I thought only my parents did that." Erica shook her head. "They think I'm thwarting them on purpose by not finding a guy and settling down with a houseful of little me's."

"Are you? Thwarting them on purpose?"

"There's barely room for me in this costume. I don't think I could fit a baby, too," Erica answered with no hesitation. She realized the lines between personal and professional were blurring in a hurry. She had to be on her guard much better than this.

"What happens after the swimming?"

Instead of shutting the conversation down like she should, or better yet, turning it back to him to mine for clues, Erica said, "The swimming is never really over. People can compete into their nineties. There're always coaching jobs and water shows. If you get in the loop, there are commercials and TV shows. Lots of options."

"But you came to me. Why, when there're all those other options?"

"Just remember," she said, naming the song for which she'd prepared the routine. At last, she was back to her cover. "It's amazing. And I can add a new dimension to it."

"That's the first song I ever wrote."

Erica looked at him over her shoulder, surprised. "But it's just now coming out."

"The timing was just never right. And of course, I've matured quite a bit since I was twelve. That helped, too."

"You wrote it when you were twelve? Wow."

"No different than your swimming. How old were you when you started?"

Erica smiled at the memory. "Four. Point taken. Still, it's a very grown up song. Very poignant, with an edge of danger."

"I reworked the lyrics last year. But the melody is still the same." He hummed a few bars. "My dad had this old tractor. That's the sound it made whenever it was about to throw a belt. One day, Adam was riding along with Dad and they lost the belt. Dad held onto Adam and they jumped off just before the tractor toppled into a creek."

"Hence the danger."

"Hence the danger." Trevor shifted around then relaxed again.

"What were the original lyrics?"

Trevor laughed and shook his head. "Oh no. It's not appropriate for mixed company."

"You can't just leave a girl hanging like that."

"Oh yes. I can." Trevor tapped her headpiece. "What about you? Did you ever dream of swimming in the Olympics?"

All the playfulness drained from Erica. She knew Trevor felt her tense because he had to shift, too. She'd had no plans to talk about her botched Olympic career.

"What girl didn't?"

* * * *

Trevor would have to be an oblivious boob to not hear sadness echoing in her voice. He wondered if she'd even realized it was there. She'd infused her tone with flippancy, but it was obvious that something had cut her deep. He should be polite and not push, but he found he really wanted to know. He wanted to understand what made her tick. His instincts told him that this was a big part of what made her into the woman she was today.

"Did you try out for the team?"

"Yep."

"So you didn't make it? I'm sure lots of people didn't make it." Trevor tried to be helpful and understanding.

She barked a humorless laugh. "You're right. Two hundred and thirty six didn't make it that year."

"There's no shame in that."

"I was one of the sixteen who did."

Trevor's eyebrows almost disappeared under his hairline when surprise coursed through him. He had an Olympic swimmer in his arms. Go figure. His brows made the return journey when he frowned. She didn't sound very happy about her accomplishment. He remembered the cramp.

"Did you get hurt?"

* * * *

Erica heard the concern in his voice and rushed to reassure him. "Nothing like that." Staring into the flickering fire with his arms tightly around her, Erica found that thinking about her brief Olympic bout wasn't so bad. Maybe she could talk about it. She'd have to leave out necessary details to keep her cover, but she found she wanted to give it a try. Maybe that would be the key to letting it go.

"I was unavoidably detained and missed an event. Needless to say, I'm not very well liked in the synchro community."

"This was what? Two, three years ago? I'm sure they'll get over it."

Erica laughed and shook her head. She'd stayed behind to take a separate flight home. When she'd gone by to apologize to her duet partner two weeks later, she'd thrown a tantrum and slapped her. Stunned, Erica had just stood there dumbfounded long after the woman had slammed the door in her face. The next day, she'd gotten her invitation for the team party. It included a warning for her not to come. That had been from their coach. It had been hard to go from darling to pariah overnight.

For her, none of the options she'd mentioned to Trevor were available. So when Trecam began to woo her into working for them, she'd gone with no hesitation. The assignments she'd had turned out to be a pretty good substitute for the swimming high she missed. Although, they were a little too infrequent. Still, they sufficed. As an added bonus, it was nice to be liked again.

Remembering Trevor's question, Erica confirmed, "Ten, actually."

"And they're not over it, yet? I say good riddance."

Erica shrugged. A whole lot easier said than done. Especially when you had to say good-bye to everyone you'd ever known in your life. She couldn't say she blamed them. They might have forgiven her if she'd been able to explain that she'd stumbled upon a bomb and had to remain immobile to keep from detonating it in the stadium. She remembered how surreal everything was while four Interpol agents had squirreled her away from the populated area and diffused the bomb.

During those four long hours, she'd made friends with the bomb techs. Not to mention gotten her first taste of the adrenaline high produced by danger. Unofficially, they'd let her help track down the culprit. Her role became more official when the evidence led back to the synchro world.

"Yes. Good riddance."

* * * *

Trevor could still hear the deep sadness in her voice. Hating that he'd been the one to bring up such unpleasant memories for her, he did what he did best. He sang the original lyrics of Just Remember for her.

"Is that . . .?" she asked then settled in to listen.

He couldn't remember the last time he'd been nervous singing for someone. But all of a sudden, he was. When she giggled at his naughty twelve year old boy logic, Trevor was glad he'd shared this with her. For the next few hours, they shared so many stories and laughs that by the time they both dropped off to sleep in the wee morning hours they were good friends.

Chapter Six

Trevor woke with a start. The first thing he noticed was that he was alone. The second was that his entire body was aching like he'd gone at least four rounds with the heavyweight champion of the world. He decided to ignore the aches and stood with care. Each joint creaked with every one of his thirty years, but he ignored that, too. Carrying her coat that was still draped around him, he stepped past the burnt out fire and outside the cave entrance to look for Erica.

The gusty wind chilled him to the bone in moments. He could just imagine how cold Erica must be since she'd been wearing a whole lot less than his own polo shirt and khakis. He ventured a few feet to one side of the cave. He hoped he wouldn't be interrupting any private moment she'd been trying to have. In fact, he needed one himself.

After handling his business he continued his search. He didn't want to get too far from the cave because he wasn't sure he could find his way back. He wanted to be there when she returned. That was the logical side of his brain. The worried side had his feet venturing to the other side to see if she were there. She wasn't.

Trying to shut the worry down, Trevor ran the conversation

they'd had the night before back through his mind. He couldn't remember ever having talked to a woman for so long and enjoying it. In fact, he never talked to people that way outside of his family and Cam. Go figure. But what amazed him was his gentlemanly behavior. If his muscles were less achy, he'd have reached around and patted himself on the back for his willpower. He'd held her all night and not made a move. Not that he hadn't wanted to. He'd lost count of the times he'd woken up ready for her until pure exhaustion had settled in. She'd seemed to sleep through his restlessness. Good thing, too. If she'd moved even the slightest bit, he knew his restraint would've flown right out the window.

Speaking of restraint, he was having a hard time keeping his worry in check. He wasn't sure how long she'd been gone, but he was starting to imagine all sorts of horrible things happening to her. He looked down the rock beach he figured they'd crossed the night before and saw nothing. He looked down the rest of the beach, but it was empty. He was just about to yell her name when he heard a scrabbling from overhead.

He looked up in time to see Erica easing her way down a steep vegetation-grown hill. He'd admired the view of long shapely legs exposed from mid-calf to hip until he saw a long scratch on one. It looked too fresh for her to have gotten last night. He admitted to himself that since she'd known him, she'd taken a pretty good battering.

"Where on earth have you been?" She dropped to the ground beside him, and he noticed that some of the leaves he'd guessed she was climbing through were attached to her. He fingered one and cocked an eyebrow. "Nice fashion statement."

She shrugged his amusement off. "They protect the suit. I hope." She spared a glance for the front of her costume then held up leafy bundle and grinned. "Breakfast."

He took the leaves from her and opened them. To his surprise, four six inch fish were nestled inside. He looked back at her, but she was already hurrying back inside the cave. Trevor followed.

"Where'd you get these?"

Erica knelt by the makeshift fire pit and worked to get it going again. "There weren't any offshore so I went inland and found a stream." She grinned up at him once an ember caught. "I don't even like fish, but I'm gonna enjoy those babies."

* * * *

Trevor set the fish down next to her and touched the scratch on the back of her thigh. "Where'd this come from?"

Erica looked at her leg in surprise. "Hmmm," was all she said and continued to stoke the fire.

"That's all you have to say. Hmmm?" Trevor sprung up and hit his head on the cave ceiling. He crouched back down. Erica went to his side to check the injury.

"You okay?"

Trevor smacked her hands away. "Stop changing the subject. Anything could've happened to you out there." He gestured to her leg. "That could get infected, and you could die. We don't know how long we're going to be here."

* * * *

Erica sat back and contemplated Trevor. How cute! He was mad at her because she'd worried him. She figured now would be a good time to tell him. Wanting to test out her memory, she'd gone exploring at first light. Good thing, because as it turned out, her memory had been fuzzy and it had taken her a while to find the road that led to a ranger's post. She marked the trail back so she'd be able to follow it with ease once she had Trevor in tow. It was on the way back that she'd discovered the stream and fish. Figuring the trek would be easier with something in their stomachs, she'd caught a few. "We'll be home, today."

Trevor stopped rubbing his head and stared at her surprised. "Today?"

"I found a road when I was fishing." He didn't need all the details. "Where there's a road, there has to be civilization." She looked at the fish. Handed them to Trevor. "You know how to clean these?"

He looked at the fish then at her like she'd just asked the stupidest question on the planet. "I grew up on a ranch. Of course I know how to clean them. But why? We should head for the road instead of wasting time with this."

Erica shook her head. "We don't know how long it'll take us to find somebody. We may need the energy."

"But it could be right over a hill or something."

She wasn't wasting time arguing over this. Erica shrugged and took the fish outside herself. Still rubbing his head, Trevor followed.

* * * *

"What are you doing?"

"If you won't clean them, I will." She pulled out her switchblade and knelt by the surf. Trevor was startled by the knife's appearance for a small moment. What irked him more was her 'I'm in charge attitude. He'd all but shaken the idea that she was his bodyguard and this wasn't helping her case. He didn't care how cute she was, he was never good at taking orders.

He squared his shoulders when he looked down at her. "That's not how you do it," was his haughty announcement. He took the fish and the knife and cleaned it with very little effort.

Erica kissed his cheek and headed back inside the cave. He watched her go and wished she'd come back. No. Trevor was glad she was gone. Because he was blushing to the roots of his hair. She didn't need to see the evidence of what she'd done to him.

* * * *

Six hours later and running on empty, Erica and Trevor trudged along the road. She looked in dismay at the setting sun and prayed that they'd gone the right way. Her memory was shaky, but she'd believed the shortest route was to head north. Except, it was possible that the road was leading them on a winding route around the island and they were wasting time and energy traveling out of their way.

"How ya doin'?" She looked over at Trevor. He did look the worse for wear. Still, he hadn't complained once and continued to put one foot in front of the other. Nor had he questioned her. For that, she was very grateful, because she had no answers to give him.

"I wouldn't mind another couple of fish. Even ones you cooked."

"Smarty." Erica made a face at him, glad their camaraderie not only lasted into the day, but that it seemed to have strengthened. Though truth be told, she wouldn't mind some of her cooking either. When she'd managed to almost decimate the first two instead of cooking them, Trevor took over the task. His cooked to perfection. Still, he'd eaten the other one too. She'd followed his lead.

Now, after trekking across the island, they were both famished and exhausted. Trevor's steps slowed to a halt. Erica stopped beside him. She didn't want to admit it, but she was happy for the reprieve.

"I don't think I can go much further." Trevor bent over, hands on his knees and sucked in air. "How many miles have we gone?"

Erica looked back down the road. Down being the operative word. They'd been traveling uphill since they'd started out. Gravity was wearing on them both. "About nine." She rubbed his back. "We should get as far as we can before we lose the daylight. We should find someone soon."

"You said that at least three hours ago."

"Well then, we're three hours closer."

Trevor shot her an irritated look, but stood and they started off again. "There's a word for people like you."

"'Optimist?'" Erica summoned up the energy to give him a smile.

"No. 'Lunatic.'" Trevor softened his comment with a playful nudge to her arm. Erica stopped dead in her tracks. Trevor halted beside her. A full smile bloomed on her face, and she pointed.

"How about 'right?'"

Trevor followed her finger with his eyes. His body sagged with relief when he saw the roof of a structure ahead. With a joyful shout, he picked Erica up and swung her around in celebration. With renewed energy they hurried toward the building.

That last mile was the quickest of the entire trek. Before they knew it, they were entering a tiny parking lot adjacent to the small ranger station. Erica was a little worried that there were no vehicles in the lot, but lights were on inside, so someone had to be around. If not, they'd at least be able to call somebody. Worst case scenario, they'd have a roof over their heads for the night.

Her idle speculation came to an abrupt end when the door was yanked open and a young ranger came barreling out, gun in hand.

"It's you!" he said running up on them.

Not stopping to think twice, Erica had him disarmed and on the ground before the poor guy knew what was what. She handed the gun to Trevor who took it without a word; the betrayal in his eyes spoke volumes. So much for convincing him that she wasn't his bodyguard.

"Hey! Lemme up! You can't do this. I'm an officer of the federal government!" The guy squirmed under Erica's weight.

"Last I checked "federal officers" didn't go about brandishing weapons in civilians' faces."

"Brandish . . . I was cleaning my gun. I saw you and Mr. Cole . . . We've been looking everywhere for you."

"That's enough, Erica." Trevor's stern command had her looking up at him in surprise. After another moment, she helped the hapless ranger up. When she saw his face, she was startled to note that he was just a kid. Just out of his teens, she'd wager.

Trevor moved to hand the weapon back to him, but Erica intercepted it. Trevor glared at her. She didn't back down from his silent challenge. Stared him down as she asked, "Who are you?"

"Ranger Watson. Jonny Watson at your service, ma'am."

The "ma'am" had her refocusing on the kid. She didn't have one foot in the grave. At her look, he backed a step away from her.

"Don't they teach you in Ranger School not to run at people with a gun unless you're planning to use it?"

"No . . . I mean . . . I was just excited. All the guys are out looking for Mr. Cole's body. I wanted to go, too, 'cause I'm a huge fan, but George said no. But I get the last laugh. Not only are you not dead, but you came to me. Let's see them not respect me now!"

Figuring the kid was more danger to himself than them, Erica handed the gun back. Still, she checked the chamber first. She figured the cat was pretty well out of the bag so she didn't bother to hide her expertise from Trevor. Jonny pulled a stained cloth from his pocket and nervously began to polish the gun. He stared at Trevor the whole time, stupid grin on his face.

"Ranger Watson. Might we go inside? It's been a long day," Trevor suggested. His calm tone did nothing to disguise his anger that she'd lied to him. If she needed her suspicions to be confirmed, they were when he followed Jonny inside the building without so much as a backward glance, never mind the usual chivalry that had accompanied them thus far. Erica searched her mind for a way to salvage this. She knew it could be done. She just wasn't sure how.

After Jonny called the team to report their appearance, he kept up a steady stream of chatter with Trevor sparing Erica from having to answer his immediate questions. Erica could tell the younger man figured himself to now be a close personal friend of Trevor Cole. All the while, Trevor would nod and give polite smiles except when he took time out to glare at her behind Jonny's back.

She was spared further when a posse of rangers returned to the office and swarmed Trevor. They told them the tail of the fisherman who'd stumbled upon the charred yacht remains before dawn that morning. Once they'd ID'd him as the owner, they'd dispatched dive teams to search for his body, but issued a vague statement to the press on purpose so they wouldn't run with a Trevor Cole is dead headline.

Trevor thanked them for their thoughtfulness. He recounted their adventure on the yacht before they'd jumped when it became evident that it was going to crash. Erica saw some evidence that he was thawing toward her when he'd included her in the statement several times. Almost immediately, he seemed to remember his anger and things would chill between the two of them again.

Erica gave a grateful smile to the rangers who draped a blanket around her shoulders. She watched Trevor watch her when she pulled her knees up under her chin and huddle beneath the blanket. He stood and paced while he continued recounting what happened to them. Erica bit back a sigh when Trevor's pacing placed him between her and the door. The last thing she wanted to do was move, but she was still assigned to protect him. Leaving him unattended near an open doorway, even surrounded by Forest Rangers wasn't an option.

Trying to be casual, Erica stood and took a new post between Trevor and the doorway. Almost without conscious thought, he moved away from both her and the door. Erica took a moment to mourn the fact that their friendship had strained so fast.

Trevor kept recounting the events, but she could tell something else was going on in his head by the slight considering frown that flitted over his features. It became apparent when he tested her by moving, with casual motion to the outside observer, back between her and the door. Erica stared him down. He stared back. She planted herself squarely in the doorway and dared him with her expression to challenge her.

A mocking smile danced on his lips before he retreated back to his original seated position. The triumphant look Trevor gave her had Erica holding her ground even though she was bone weary and her legs were about to collapse at any moment. Still, she wasn't about to give him the satisfaction of leaving the doorway so he could take that spot. Judging by the expression on his face, she knew that's just what he planned to do.

Jonny looked between the two of them. Erica could sense that he saw the power struggle between her and Trevor, but did not understand the cause. "Mr. Cole. The boat is here. Whenever you're ready it'll return you both to the mainland."

Erica shot Trevor a surprised look. Boat? He wanted to get back on a boat after the last one had almost killed him? And what about the choppers she'd heard overhead? Oh no. The ranger had to be mistaken.

Erica touched Trevor's shoulder. The icy look he shot her way made her drop the offending hand. Still, she pressed on with her quest. "Wouldn't the chopper be faster?"

Trevor leveled a cold stare at her for a moment then flashed his rock star smile around the tiny station. "Nothing like getting right back in the saddle. Eh?" He rose again from his seat. Erica caught the stiffening of his joints, and he addressed her at last. "Ready?"

At least he wasn't planning to leave her behind. Not eager to antagonize this thin show of good will, she exchanged her ready retort that she goes where he goes for a quiet, "Yes," and followed him to the shore. She had to figure out a way to rebuild some figment of a relationship between them. Even if the friendship that once budded between them was now out of the question. Given the attraction between them, it had to be for the best that it'd been nipped in the bud. Still, she had a job to do. She couldn't do it if he kicked her out of his life.

Her steps slowed while a germ of an idea began to take shape. Putting it into action, Erica stumbled against Jonny. He righted her like she'd expected and never even noticed when she swiped his cell phone from his belt. Although, Trevor studied her like he knew she was up to something.

* * * *

The closer he got to the tiny speedboat, the more he was beginning to feel that maybe the chopper was a better idea. No sooner had the idea formed than he'd clamped down on it. If he didn't want to fear boats the rest of his life he had to get back on one. Immediately. He suspected Erica needed the same. Even though he didn't want to care if she were able to conquer her fear, he did. But he'd be darned if he let her know that.

He glanced at her behind him. She followed like she had nothing more urgent on her mind than putting one foot in front of the other. Maybe the crash hadn't scared her like it had him. Then he reminded himself. This is what she does. The crash had to be all in a day's work for her. He snorted. How had he managed to be saddled with a bodyguard that he didn't want?

Trevor chose a seat inside the tiny boat cabin. It was one thing to get back on the boat. It was another to see them racing over the waves in actuality. Like he'd expected, Erica followed him inside. Unwanted compassion filled him when he saw her look around and choose to stand for the ride back because there were no seats between the one he'd selected and the doorway. There was no way she wasn't exhausted. He was shaky with fatigue himself, and he hadn't spent near the amount of energy she had. Without trying to make a big deal about it, he moved to another seat. He saw the grateful surprise in her eyes when she sat in his vacated seat. For a moment, Trevor forgot to be angry with her. He liked her. That was genuine. He wanted their budding friendship back. Except what kind of friendship could be built on lies?

"All set? We'll have you home in no time," Jonny announced in a cheerful voice. The man hadn't strayed far from Trevor's side since they'd reached the ranger station. More often than not, he had the humor for these things, but he was too exhausted to think, much less make small talk with the guy.

"You mind if she and I have some time to chat?" Trevor asked when Jonny settled into his own seat inside the cabin. Erica raised a wary eyebrow. Jonny looked between the two of them and hopped up. He swayed a bit when the captain put them underway, but headed for the door. He shot Trevor a wolfish grin.

"Chat. Of course." He pounded Trevor's fist with his own then left them by themselves in the cabin.

Trevor saw the hope in Erica's eyes. He hardened his. "I couldn't take anymore." He could've been the biggest cad on the planet the way light faded from her eyes at his explanation.

"I understand." She turned away to stare out the portholes at the water speeding by them.

Trevor wanted to say something else but he didn't know what so he left things alone.

Chapter Seven

The ride back to the mainland took not even twenty minutes. With things strained between them like they were, the ride could've been a week. Hidden in the blanket's folds, Erica texted her plan to Jason. Since she was using someone else's cell phone, she knew he wouldn't respond. She could just hope he'd gotten her message and set things up for her.

At long last, Jonny opened the door to announce their arrival at the shore. Erica glanced out the window when lights began to flash. Trevor groaned when he noticed the paparazzi swarming the dock they would use to disembark.

Trevor looked at his torn, sweat stained clothes. "My mom is going to love these photos."

Hoping a common enemy would repair their bond a bit, Erica offered, "You want some of the blanket?"

Trevor considered her for a long moment then shook his head. "Ready?"

Erica stood on shaky limbs and dropped Jonny's phone in the chair he'd vacated and wrapped herself tighter in the blanket. Satisfied Trevor never noticed her action, she headed for the door.

Erica noticed that Trevor didn't complain when she stuck

close to him on the dock. In fact, he snaked an arm about her waist and guided her through the throng of crazed reporters and photographers. Jonny followed the best he could, but got pushed back in the wild shuffle. He settled for yelling, "Call me!" The boat captain just shook his head and continued working in his logbook.

Together, Trevor and Erica made their way up the dock to the parking lot. Trevor froze in surprise. Erica looked at him. His rock star smile looked more brittle than usual.

"What's wrong?" Erica pretended not to know.

Trevor turned to smile down at her like that had been his intent all along. Hyperaware of all the cameras still snapping away, he whispered, "My car is gone."

"What?" Erica looked around the parking lot pretending to ascertain the veracity of his statement. "How is that possible? Don't you have assigned spots or something?"

Smile still in place, "Yes. And mine is empty."

"Hmmm." She looked back at him. "Well, if you can suspend your hate of me for a bit, I can give you a ride."

Trevor stared at her for a long time. "How'd you pull this off?"

Erica feigned a hurt innocence. "I'm a one woman operation. How could I possibly manage something like this?" She laid down the beginnings of her new cover story. "Besides, I've been with you the whole time. Think how good I must be to arrange this without you knowing."

Erica held his gaze. Trevor never blinked while he studied her. At last he relented. "I accept your offer."

Erica nodded and led the way to her lavender VW bug. She expected him to comment on her extremely girly vehicle, but he held his tongue. It served to remind her how far they had to go to repair their friendship. The fact that he'd stopped at the navy BMW next to it and raised his eyebrows when he realized he was wrong told her she'd surprised him. Once they were settled inside, she lost no time putting some distance between them and the paparazzi. After she'd lost the last of their relentless pursuers, Erica spared a look at Trevor. She was encouraged when she saw the impressed expression on his face. She seized her opportunity.

"I'm really sorry I misled you. But you have to admit,

someone is after you. You need protection."

"The police are already on the case."

Erica pulled over so she could turn to face him. "It's commendable that you have this deep rooted humility. In fact, I'm sure it's part of the reason you're so successful. But I don't want to see it get you killed."

"It's not going to get me killed."

"No? Your yacht exploded and someone detonated a bomb they sent to you."

Trevor stared stubbornly through the windshield, not giving her any clue to what he was thinking. She waited for him to look at her. Erica reached over to squeeze his hand. "When are you going to admit that you need protection?"

* * * *

Trevor studied their hands. After a moment, he pulled away from her. "I'd like to get home, now."

He turned to look out the passenger side window, shutting her out. Erica sighed and eased the car back into traffic while Trevor mulled over the last few days. She and Cam were right. He did need protection. It killed him to admit it and he was sure the pygmies would be arriving at any moment, but he also had to be honest with himself. He would not be alive right now if he hadn't had help. He liked Erica, but that was also a problem. She'd be more distraction than woodwork. And as a one woman operation, she couldn't have the resources that Trecam had. He needed this thing resolved fast as possible. He would call Caitlyn first thing in the morning. That settled, Trevor realized they were turning into his driveway. Erica parked at his front door.

Trevor had every intention of bidding her farewell in the car. Of course, Erica had other ideas. She bounded around and to the door while he got his keys out. He was strangely torn when he located the correct key on his ring. She had saved his life. But she'd also deceived him. A general rule he lived by, don't keep anyone around he can't trust. That was one of the reasons that he'd been able to remain grounded even among the nonsense his chosen career generated. Except, deep down, he knew he could trust her — with his life.

"Thanks, Erica. It was . . . an adventure . . . meeting you."

"If you change your mind . . ."

"I won't." Trevor gave her his rock star smile, but it had an obvious tinge of sadness to it. He pushed open the door, but Erica held him back.

"At least let me sweep it, first."

Trevor sighed, but stepped back allowing her to enter. Trevor waited about thirty seconds before he started feeling silly. This was his house. His sanctuary. It was safe. The first thing he noticed was the chill. Without giving it a second thought, he turned the thermostat up to its limit. He wanted the place heated fast.

He wanted to go check on Erica. He was curious to see her reaction to his home. No sooner had the notion formed than he shook it away. He was going to say good-bye to Erica for good in just a few moments. He wanted the break to be a clean one. He needed it to be clean.

Erica's steps faltered when she saw him in the foyer flipping through his mail. He sensed her annoyance before she even opened her mouth. He was surprised when the rebuke he expected didn't come.

"You have a great place. A little cold, but nice."

"Thanks. And I just turned up the thermostat. It'll be back to normal in here soon."

Erica frowned. "You mean it's not always like this? Did you turn the air on before you left?"

Trevor shrugged, not understanding her interest in his home's temperature. He was getting to the point where he could not even think beyond a bath, his bed and a meal, not necessarily in that order.

Erica took a look around again. "We have to get out of here."

"What? No way. I'm beat."

"Head for the door. Now!"

He heard the urgency in her whisper just before he heard the rattle. Lots and lots of rattles. And hisses.

Trevor sucked in a surprised breath when snakes of every size and color slithered out from under his furniture. Erica clutched at Trevor's arm while she stared at the reptiles heading for them. At last, she gathered her wits and reached for the door. Trevor snatched her arm back just as a cobra snapped at it.

* * * *

Shaken, Erica needed to take a moment. Trevor grabbed a nearby coat rack and cleared a path to the door. Erica got herself together long enough to yank the door open so they could both flee. Trevor pulled the door closed behind them.

Erica grabbed his arm and hustled them away from the house. She didn't stop until they were halfway down the driveway. Freaked out, Erica tried to walk off her fear. She so didn't do snakes. Trevor saw how upset she was and pulled her into his embrace. At first she tried to resist. She was supposed to be comforting him. Not the other way around. Some bodyguard she was turning out to be.

"We're safe, Erica. Everything's okay."

She pulled away from him in anger. "How can you say that? Someone wants you dead. No. Everything's not okay!"

"It couldn't have been easy getting all those snakes. The police will track him." He tried to pull her close again, but she danced out of his grasp.

"When they're not busy tracking all the murderers who've already succeeded." A bit calmer, she whirled on him. "What's the big deal? Why won't you let me protect you?"

"No, Erica."

"It doesn't make any sense."

"Leave it alone."

"But . . ." Erica's retort was cut short when a pair of headlights swept over them and up the driveway. Wondering who could be stopping by this late, she took up a defensive posture between Trevor and the intruder.

Trevor brushed by her. "Give it a rest. It's just Cam." He headed for the sedan when it stopped short of the main house. Cam rolled down his window. Even in the darkening of nightfall, Erica could see the relief on the other man's face when he saw for himself that Trevor was okay.

"Need a lift up to the house?" Cam called while Trevor approached. "What are you two doing out here anyway? After your little adventure, I'd think you'd both be pooped."

Trevor leaned in the window. "We've got a little problem."

"You lost your key? No worries." He held up a set of keys. "I figured you might have. When I heard you'd been found, I rushed them right over."

Erica leaned against the back door. She overheard the emotion brimming in the man's voice and didn't want to intrude. Somehow she knew without a doubt that he was the one who'd brought in Trecam. Though she couldn't imagine him and Caitlyn being good friends like her boss implied. Though, something about the red stubble on his chin tickled her subconscious.

"Actually, we've been inside. Someone left me another present. Snakes. Lots and lots of snakes."

After her crash course in all things Trevor, Erica was able to hear how hard he had to work to keep his tone flippant. For the first time, she was able to detect that the man was afraid. With good reason. Whoever was holding this grudge against him was without a doubt serious.

"Neither of us have a phone, so could you . . ." Trevor didn't even get his sentence finished before Cam was on his police radio calling in backup. Relieved, Trevor squatted by his friend's window and rested his forehead against the door. "And my car's gone, too. It wasn't at the dock where I left it."

"It's in the impound," Cam informed Trevor who looked at him with a frown.

"What? Why?"

"Another bomb threat was phoned in. We swept it for obvious explosives, but we took it in to check it more in depth. So far, we've found nothing. You should get it back in a couple days. After everything . . . we're not taking any chances."

Trevor nodded and stared dumbly at his friend. Erica rested a comforting hand on his shoulder. Without thinking, he squeezed it with gratitude. The satisfied look that flitted over Cam's face had Trevor's heckles rising.

"Son of a . . . it was you, wasn't it?" He saw Erica tense beside him. She moved to look at Cam closer not understanding Trevor's accusation. "You hired her, didn't you?" Trevor shrugged away from Erica and began to pace in his fury.

* * * *

Cam locked eyes with Erica. He wasn't surprised that he didn't see any shock on her features at Trevor's pronouncement. So he must have already figured out she was his bodyguard.

Still, something didn't jibe. Trevor hadn't mentioned Trecam. Was it possible Erica had managed to salvage part of her cover? It wouldn't surprise him. She had to be a smart cookie if Caitlyn chose her. Behind Trevor's back, she gave him a slight shake of her head indicating he should bite back the defense that sprung to his lips. He let Trevor take the lead.

"Well I guess I should be grateful at least that you didn't bring in Caitlyn." Trevor nailed Erica with a look. "You must have one heck of a one woman operation for Cam to call you."

Cam fought a smile. His suspicions had been spot on. Erica was good. One woman operation, huh? He could live with that. Better yet, Trevor might just be able to live with it. And Cam wanted his friend to live. Frustrated that he couldn't just pop out of his car and knock some sense into the man, Cam let Erica do it.

"You're being unreasonable, Trevor. You have been this whole time." She gestured toward his snake-filled house. "You obviously need some help here. I can protect you. If you'd just let me."

* * * *

Trevor whirled and bellowed, "I will not fear this guy!" Sick of people interfering in his life, Trevor conveniently forgot his earlier vow to call Caitlyn himself. He'd do what needed to be done. He just needed them to get off his back about it. If he wanted to walk around without a bodyguard, that was his business.

"Look. Both of you have had a rough day. Get out of here. I'll take care of things. Go get some rest and we'll get your statements later."

Trevor sensed their gazes when he turned toward his house just to stop short. He blew out a breath of frustration when his missing car crossed his mind. Resigned he faced them again.

"I don't have a car."

"Ride with me," Erica offered.

Trevor studied her for a long moment. The woman just wouldn't give up. But he was running out of options. He knew a fight with Cam was inevitable if he hitched a ride with him. So Trevor came up with a compromise. He shook his head and held out his hand. "I'll drive."

"That's not necessary."

Trevor shrugged. "I've already walked eighteen miles today. What's another five?"

Erica chased after him. "Fine. You drive. Let's just get out of here."

Trevor stopped and took the keys Erica handed him. He saluted Cam then headed for her car. Erica fell in step behind him.

"Take care of him," Cam called to Erica under his breath when she passed. The sentiment still reached Trevor's ears. Like he needed someone coddling him day in and day out. His anger rose another notch.

"I'm trying to."

Trevor barely waited for Erica to get her door closed before he took off down the driveway. He swerved on his manicured lawn to pass Cam and didn't spare a backward glance at the destruction he'd left in his wake.

Erica gripped the dashboard while she fumbled for her seatbelt. "I guess asking you to slow down would be pointless, huh?"

Trevor ignored her. He squealed around corners and ran red lights while he sped toward his destination. He couldn't believe it. He had a crazy man after him and the last thing he needed was his supposed best friend conspiring against him. He spared a glance at Erica. Especially with her. Trevor took a little satisfaction when he careened around a bus and turned right just in front of it causing Erica to stomp on an imaginary brake. He was thrilled that she realized that he and only he was the one to control his life. Since they'd met, he'd had no doubt that she'd been in control.

Still, he had to give a grudging admission that he was impressed she hadn't said anything more during their wild ride across town. The women he'd known would be nagging his ears off right now with demands to slow the vehicle. Not Erica. Other than her fruitless attempts to hit a brake pedal that wasn't there, she let him do what he was going to do.

None too soon, Trevor screeched to a halt in a small driveway nestled in an understated residential area. He announced his name in a small intercom, and the tall bushes slid apart revealing more driveway beyond. Erica looked at Trevor, her amazement obvious.

* * * *

"What is this place?"

For a long moment, she didn't think Trevor was going to answer her. At last, he said in a gruff tone, "Pine Hills."

Pine Hills? She'd heard rumors that it existed, but no one could ever confirm it. Because things stayed rather low key and legal, there'd been no real reason to look for it. The estate was a secluded hideaway where the mega rich and celebrities could escape the public for a while. Erica shouldn't be surprised that Trevor picked Pine Hills instead of a hotel. Since he fit both categories of their clientele, it made sense that he'd go there to get himself together.

"Three twenty two," the disembodied voice replied to Trevor. He nodded and drove inside. The hedges slid closed behind them.

It was obvious Trevor was still not inclined to make small talk so Erica busied herself with studying the layout of the place. She was impressed with what she saw. Cottages lined both sides of the perfectly paved street. Well maintained lawns surrounded each cottage along with tall hedges, affording the occupants total privacy to the side and Erica supposed the back of each cottage.

All too soon, Trevor pulled up in front of a cottage marked three twenty two and climbed from behind the wheel. Erica scrambled out after him.

"I trust you can find your way out."

Erica faced him with a casual shrug. "I'll find my way out when you're ready to go."

"You're not staying here, Erica. We're done. I no longer need your services." He strode up to the door and punched in a security code. Without a sound, the door eased open. "If I did, I'm perfectly capable of finding someone . . . more suitable."

Erica didn't let the barb find its mark. The only reason she hadn't been "suitable" so far is because he'd fought her every step of the way.

"Nice knowin' ya." Trevor stepped inside and closed the door in her face.

Erica stood on the tiny porch for a long moment weighing her options. True, it was a technicality, but since he hadn't hired her, he couldn't fire her either. She'd gotten a clear directive from Cam who she now had no doubt was her client that she was to take care of him. With a shrug and a sigh she headed back to her car. Erica pulled an overnight bag from the trunk and slammed the lid to help rid herself of her frustration. She trudged back up on the porch and tried to make herself comfortable in front of his door. Not the easiest thing to do in the brisk air, but she'd manage.

* * * *

Trevor scrubbed his hands over his face. He thought he'd never be able to get rid of her. He had to give her credit. She was tenacious. He jumped when he heard her car door slam. She was really going to leave him. Isn't that what you wanted, a voice in his head sneered. He chose not to respond. Trevor pushed himself off the door. He didn't want to hear her drive away. He headed for the shower. He hoped that cleaning his aching body would keep his mind off why he felt so alone all of a sudden.

When he stepped from the shower, he was glad to have rid himself of the dirt and grime of his ordeal at last. Trevor padded toward the kitchen. Exhaustion should've had him flat on his back, but he found that he was still pretty wired. Figuring food was just what the doctor ordered he set out to see what sounded good. The facility kept their kitchens stocked for unannounced visits like his. He knew the slight delay in his cottage assignment had been because they'd needed to consult their list to see which one was ready.

Trevor wasn't disappointed. He opened the refrigerator to a wide selection of choices. Unbidden, his mind wandered back to Erica. He wondered if she'd gotten home, yet, if she'd eaten. Now that he'd bathed and was more like himself, Trevor regretted how he'd treated her. She was just trying to help. She couldn't know about the pygmies. And if he had to deal with them, it was at least going to be by his invitation. His appetite fled so he settled for grabbing a bottle of water from the refrigerator and headed back toward his bed.

When he passed through the foyer, he looked at the door where he'd last seen Erica. A frown creased his brow when he caught a glimpse of the rear of a car parked out front. Surely, not . . .

Trevor went to the front door and peeked out the window.

Her car was still parked right where he'd left it. He couldn't see anybody in it. Sure she was slouched down in the seat, he keyed in the door code and ripped it open intent to send her on her way.

He stopped short when he almost tripped over her figure huddled in front of the door. Alarm zipped through him. What had happened? Was she okay? Concern shredded away the last of his anger when he couldn't even detect that she was breathing. He knelt beside her.

"Erica!" Trevor lifted her up to cradle her in his arms. Even in her big, battered coat, she was shivering from the cold.

"Trevor? Is everything okay?" She tried to stand, but he held her tight. He noted her lethargic movements and wasn't sure if he wanted to kiss her or scold her for staying out here like this. Still trying to protect him whether he wanted her to or not. It was about time he repaid the favor.

Trevor stood then swept her up to carry her inside the cottage and kicked the door closed with his foot. In the back of his mind, he marveled that her hair seemed to be the lone thing to emerge from their ordeal unscathed. It looked just the same as it had when they'd first met.

"What are you doing? Put me down." She squirmed, but held on tight. It worried Trevor that there wasn't very much behind her fight. Then again, she had to be bone weary like he was.

"Stubborn woman," he growled when he deposited her, coat and all in the oversized Jacuzzi tub. He noticed belatedly that she had a bag clenched in her fist when he tried to rid her of the coat.

"Stop it, Trevor." She smacked his hands away. He retreated just far enough to turn on the water.

"You're about frozen to the bone. Get warmed up," he commanded with more sharpness than he'd intended. She tried to stand, but he pushed her back down with a firm hand. "You'll stay here tonight. We'll figure tomorrow out . . . tomorrow." He did manage to get the coat off of her before it got soaked through and laid it over the sink. Seeing her costume again did things to his libido that shouldn't have been possible in his current run through the ringer state. He retreated for the door.

"Trevor?" He paused long enough to look at her. "Thank you."

He gave her a curt nod. "I'm going to scare up some

dinner." He fled from the bathroom before she could get a good look at the front of his sweatpants.

* * * *

Beginning to relax and thaw under the luxurious hot water, Erica rethought her decision to spend the night on the porch. She was acting almost as stupid as he was. Her car would've at least had heat, but it was too far from her client, and she didn't know what was behind the cottage.

She swiveled in the tub so the hot water gushed over her head and pulled the pins from her hairpiece. She'd slid the last bobby pin out and tossed the thing on the floor with gratitude. She'd inspect it for damage later, but she was dying to get out of her costume.

First, Erica coated her hair with conditioner, then shimmied her way out of the clingy fabric and winced when her chaffed skin met the hot water. The costumes weren't designed for comfort, but it hadn't bothered her to spend an hour, and no more than that, in one. However, by her calculation, she been in this one for the last thirty-two hours. And the conditions she'd worn it through had been much more rigorous than the pool decks to which it was accustomed. Erica was saddened, but not surprised to see the frays and holes in the fabric. One solitary crystal in the front managed to survive intact. Determined not to mourn the poor costume, Erica wrung out the fabric and laid it to rest on the side of the tub with a gentle hand. Her nose clips were still tangled in the fabric where it had rested on her hipbones so she pulled those free and dropped them into a side pocket of her bag.

She turned her attention to rinsing the gel out of her hair. The conditioner had worked its magic allowing her fingers to work the hot water through her tresses while Erica tried to make heads or tails of this sudden stay of execution. She didn't for one minute think Trevor'd changed his mind, but he could've carried her to her car just as easily. Too tired to work through anything else tonight, she focused on getting all the grit off her body. With her hair for the most part gel free, Erica plugged the drain and added the Epsom salt she'd learned to keep with her to the water. She turned the jets on and laid her head on the tub to enjoy it.

* * * *

Trevor always tended to snack when he cooked and this time was no exception. By the time the vegetable stew he'd thrown together was ready to serve, he'd found that the edge was gone off his appetite. He hadn't heard another peep from Erica so he let the stew simmer and wandered into the living room. The cottage was fully equipped, and Trevor found himself booting up the laptop to check his e-mail.

He returned a couple of frantic ones from his family. Guilt settled on his shoulders that he'd only just now thought about them. He should've at least called his parents straight away. Now that he had remembered them, he wasn't all that eager to have the talk he knew it would turn into. He'd call them after he'd rested and gotten his wits about him. He was going to need them because he was sure his mother already knew that an "unidentified woman" had been with him. Trevor wasn't up to reassuring her. He didn't have the answers for the questions he knew she'd ask anyway. That thought had him opening up a search engine to find out more about the mysterious Erica Kellogg.

It didn't take him long. The Internet was loaded with news item after news item about her indiscretion at the Olympics. She'd told him that she'd been detained. The news reported that despite several attempts by her coach and teammates she'd remained locked in the locker room and refused to come out. For four hours, she'd kept it up. The reporter indicated that unnamed sources blamed a fight Erica'd had with her duet partner over a boy and she decided to be a diva and screw the whole team.

Trevor frowned at that. He couldn't imagine Erica ever pulling a stunt like that. She'd shown herself to be far too level-headed with a one track mind. It occurred to him that the incident was years ago. He was positive her current occupation had matured her. Still, he had trouble believing the report. He didn't have any trouble, however, believing that she'd been a pariah in the synchro community ever since. Because she'd missed both her duet and team routine, an alternate had swum. A badly prepared alternate from what he could glean. It allowed the Russian team to sweep by the USA to claim the gold. The incident threw the whole US team off so hard that they didn't even get a bronze medal in those games.

That had been a direct quote from one of her teammates, and he suspected, her duet partner if the bitterness he read into it could be trusted.

Speaking of trusted, Trevor realized that he had yet to see a photo of the Erica Kellogg the print had done such a wonderful job of maligning. It wasn't long before a younger Erica was smiling at him from the laptop screen. Trevor's breath hitched when he recognized the suit. It was her all right. He had to admit that she'd filled out very well since that photo had been snapped. When he could drag his eyes away from Erica to study the girl who'd been her duet partner he figured that he'd found the source of all those bitter quotes. Even the thick layers of makeup couldn't hide her insecurity. Erica's obvious joy overshadowed the poor girl even in a photo.

"Whatcha doing?" the live, grown up version asked when she tentatively entered the living room. Realizing that she was walking on eggshells because of him, Trevor gave her a small smile. He almost didn't recognize her. He'd gotten used to seeing her hair molded to her head under that little sparkly thing. He was certain he preferred her like this. With her thick chestnut tresses swinging in inviting waves around her shoulders. He hadn't guessed she had so much of it either. He wasn't sure how, but she looked softer, too.

He also liked the tank top that didn't quite skim the top of her baggy knit pants. Just when he'd figured she couldn't look any sexier than she had in that costume, she proved him wrong. He wondered what she'd do if he went and slid his hands up under her tank. It would be interesting to see where things went from there. He couldn't even seem to remember his anger. But he was going to be a gentleman if it killed him—and it very well might.

"Checking e-mail." He closed the browser and set the computer down. "Hungry?"

"Trevor, I—"

"Tomorrow." He rose and headed back toward the kitchen. Erica hesitated a moment then followed. Trevor served them both up a hearty bowl of stew, and they sat to eat their first meal together.

The atmosphere was strained between them until Trevor couldn't deny his pride any longer at her enjoyment of the stew. His chest puffed out as he spooned a second helping into her bowl before she'd asked. She gave him a tentative smile then laughed.

"Aren't you the little peacock?" She took another bite. "A peacock who can cook for me any day."

He accepted the compliment with a smile. Then the tension between them seemed to melt away, and remnants of their budding friendship began to resurface. It wasn't long before he was having trouble keeping his eyes open. He could see that Erica was in the same boat. Together, they cleared away the dishes then headed off to separate bedrooms where they bid each other good night in the hallway.

Chapter Eight

It was almost two the next afternoon before Trevor was rested enough to climb out of bed to stay. The first few hours, he'd been out like a light. Once he'd begun to get caught up on his rest, his subconscious mind took the liberty of wandering to all sort of places where it had no business. Its favorite hideout turned out to be with Erica.

He wondered if she'd slept in her tank and pants. He wanted to know what would happen if he went across the hall and slid those pants off. Would she protest or would she undress him? His mind dwelled on her undressing him. He longed to feel her graceful fingers linking behind his head pulling him close for a kiss—and much more.

Easing up on an elbow, Trevor realized that the problem hadn't been confined to his mind. He couldn't remember the last time he'd been so ready and eager for a woman. Especially one not even in sight. A soft splash caught his attention. Glad for the distraction, he got up to investigate.

The door to Erica's room was open. Her bag at the foot of the bed was the sole evidence that she'd even been there. He heard a splash again. The bathroom door was open ruling out the possibility that she was taking a bath. He ventured to the living room on his way to the kitchen and stopped short. He hadn't noticed it before, but just off the back patio was a large pool with diving boards at one end. He knew in his gut that was where he'd find her.

Trevor stepped out on the patio and had the pleasure of watching Erica swim for the first time. If she was gorgeous on land, it paled to what she was in the water. She didn't even have any music playing. That he could hear, anyway, but that didn't stop him from feeling the melody she created to the core of his being.

He watched while one leg rose from the water. Then the other joined it before swinging around and spinning them both back down. She exploded out of the water almost to her thighs, posed her arms, and then sunk again. One arm led the way to the surface where it swiveled and twisted then was followed by her body. Trevor couldn't figure out how, but she flowed across the pool's surface with both arms dancing above her head.

He ventured closer to get a better look. She lay down in a crawl stroke for a bit then piked and her legs took the stage. Each movement was placed with such expert precision that he couldn't look away. He found himself holding his breath while she stayed under longer and longer. When his lungs were about to burst, she lowered a leg back to the surface of the water and rolled up. An arm followed the trajectory of the leg.

Feeling as if the music was going to burst through his soul, Trevor rushed back inside the cottage and sat at the baby grand piano. He angled the bench to keep watching Erica while his fingers danced over the keys bringing her melody to life.

* * * *

Erica could almost imagine she heard a lovely ballad playing every time she surfaced. She knew it had to be her imagination because it was the perfect complement to every move she made. Since she'd been trying to swim out her frustrations it wasn't possible that the music was anywhere except inside her head. For that she was grateful. She hadn't wanted to share something so personal with anyone.

She'd woken up with an acute awareness that Trevor was just across the hall with his rippling muscles and taut backside.

Needing to rid herself of the excess energy those thoughts produced, she was delighted to discover a pool just out back. She hadn't wasted any time in digging out her emergency swim kit where she kept an extra suit, goggles and nose clip at all times. One never knew when one would need to swim. And she'd needed to swim.

Erica gasped in surprise when she surfaced facing the open patio door and saw him playing the piano while watching her. Her dismay was palpable when the music she'd heard stopped along with his fingers.

"Don't stop. It's beautiful," Trevor encouraged through the doorway. He kept his fingers poised and ready.

"Trevor? You're awake." Erica wondered just how long he'd been watching her. And playing that song. She'd never heard it before, but she knew it'd be a dream to choreograph.

"That was amazing." Trevor came outside and squatted on the deck confirming her fears. "I've never seen anything quite like it."

Erica pulled off her nose clip and placed her goggles on top of her head. She wanted to see him clearly. He sounded sincere, but she wanted to be certain. "What's the name of the song you were playing? It was lovely."

"I thought you'd like to name it. After all, I was just playing what you swam."

Erica's eyebrows shot up. Playing what she swam? She'd never even heard of such a thing. She remembered all the music she'd choreographed. Maybe, just maybe, it was possible for a musician to work the other way. Write the music to the routine. After all, that's how people scored movies. And Trevor was a talented musician. Still, she couldn't wrap her mind around the fact that he'd written a song for her.

"I'll defer that honor to you." Erica whip kicked to the edge of the pool. She paused to eggbeater and tucked her nose clip in the bottom of her suit so she wouldn't drop it.

Trevor smiled. A genuine one. He held up a solemn hand. "I humbly accept." A puzzled look settled on his face. "How do you stay up like that?"

Erica glanced at her legs where they churned water just below the surface. "Eggbeater. Wanna find a suit so I can teach you?"

Trevor shook his head and stood up. The way he backed away made her realize it wasn't just the ocean he feared. "Maybe later," he responded. "Are you hungry?"

Erica's mind hadn't progressed to food, but now that he'd mentioned it, she discovered that she could definitely eat. She'd already been in the water for over an hour. The workout had left her famished like always.

"I wouldn't say no." She hoisted herself out to the deck. Trevor went stock still. She followed his gaze to her chest where both nipples were standing at attention. Perhaps she hadn't swum long enough. A voice whispered that forever wouldn't be long enough as long as he was about. Erica wished she'd brought out a towel. Anything to hide the effect he had on her. She settled for wrapping her arms around herself. "Cold out here."

Trevor met her eyes with a small smile. "Go get warm. I'll see to breakfast."

Glad he'd given her an out even though she knew he knew she wasn't cold, Erica hurried into the cottage.

* * * *

Trevor remained on the patio for a moment. The problem he'd thought he'd gotten rid of just came back. He focused his mind on anything that wouldn't remind him of her. A task much easier said than done seeing how everything was starting to remind him of her. Figuring some type of physical exertion was needed Trevor glanced at the pool. He shuddered. He wasn't that desperate—yet. He remembered his offer of food. Now that he could handle. He headed inside the cottage to the kitchen. He was very proud of himself when he never even glanced in the direction of the bathroom where he knew she must be.

Trevor patted himself on the back. The busy work of preparing their meal had gone a long way toward helping him forget about his reactions to Erica. Then she had to go and appear in the kitchen after a quick shower and wearing those sexy sweats again. All his hard work just about came undone. She countered the effect by jumping in to help with the preparations. A teasing rapport developed between the two of them while they moved around in perfect harmony. She was content to let him handle the actual cooking, but turned out to be great at anticipating what he needed next and when he was finished so the kitchen was tidied up as they went.

When they sat down to their meal, Trevor surprised them both by offering up a quick prayer of thanks. He wasn't sure what had come over him. He never prayed around other people. The people he encountered in his line of work tended to be pretty uncomfortable with the reminder that God was in control. Generally, Trevor let it slide, but with Erica he was confident he could show her who he was. On some level, he supposed he hoped it would scare her away. When she tacked on a scripture to his prayer he knew his plan had backfired.

* * * *

When they finished their meal, Erica could feel the somber mood settling around them. They had some unfinished business to iron out. She knew that neither of them was eager to broach the subject, and was happy to let Trevor take the lead.

Erica was surprised when he said, "After seeing you swim, I'd love to have you in the show."

Had he changed his mind? Erica's rising hopes began to plummet. She prompted, "But?"

"I can't have you be my bodyguard."

"Can't have me or anybody?" Erica probed, working hard to keep the hurt at bay.

* * * *

"Anybody." Trevor paused to think. "And especially you." He saw the wounded expression in her eyes and caught her hand in his even while she was trying to pull away. "You know it's too complicated, don't you?"

"You need to stay alive and I can make that happen. There's nothing complicated about that."

Without bothering to rethink his actions, Trevor leaned forward and claimed her lips with his. They were every bit as soft as he'd imagined — softer. She tasted like the fresh strawberries and the Belgium waffles they'd just had and like . . . Erica. Electricity started zinging up and down his spine before igniting a heat that settled in his groin. It was so right, kissing this woman except it was also . . . wrong. Trevor stopped concentrating on what was going on with him long enough to notice that she wasn't kissing him back. He pulled out every trick he knew all to no avail.

* * * *

Erica tried every trick she knew to sit there dispassionately while Trevor's clever mouth loved her closed lips. The electricity that was flying around her body caught her by surprise. She'd never been so attracted to anyone in her life. And never had that attraction had such high stakes behind it. She was glad for the sensible cotton bra she wore. It would do a much better job of hiding her straining nipples than the suit she'd just hung in the bathroom. And the heat pooling in her belly wouldn't be noticeable. But her toes, she had to get them to uncurl. Why hadn't she put on shoes?

Trevor stopped moving. He broke off the contact to look at her. Knowing she needed to attack so he wouldn't see how he affected her, Erica said, "Feel better?"

Erica saw her ploy worked when he shuttered his expression. But not before she caught a glimpse of wounded male ego. He popped up from his seat to pace. Erica exhaled the breath she'd been holding then leaned forward to rest her arms on her knees. Since her body still wasn't cooperating, she had a bit more hiding to do.

* * * *

He turned to look at her, envious of her calm. Hadn't she felt anything? Had he misread the signs between them that badly? There she was, sitting in the chair with her hands loosely clasped just beyond her knees. Then he noticed her toes. They were gripping the carpet like her life depended on it. Trevor fought back his smile.

Her question killed any triumph he had at his discovery that she wasn't so immune to him like she pretended. Once he'd dissuaded her from this whole bodyguard thing, he'd pursue that tiny thread, but for now . . .

Trevor moved his chair and sat directly in front of her, mirroring her posture. He needed her to understand. But he was going to leave out all mention of the pygmies.

"I can't swim."

Erica frowned. He could see her confusion. "What does that . . . ?"

"After Jordan and I . . . He went back in the water. I wouldn't." Trevor looked away. He didn't want to admit his greatest failure to her. But he knew she wouldn't give up this bodyguard nonsense until he made her understand. Now that he'd gotten a little rest, he'd decided it was still a bit premature to call Caitlyn. "I was too afraid. Now, I just can't . . . I've taken lessons over the years, but it always ends with me embarrassing myself."

Trevor looked Erica in the eye. He needed to be sure she got it. "That's what fear does to you. Once you give in to it, it'll always be with you."

He saw the understanding dawn in her brown eyes. He was ready for any argument she may have. Heck, he'd already made most of them to himself.

"You have homeowners insurance, right?"

Okay. So she'd lost him with that one. He shrugged. "Yeah. Why?"

"Well, what is that except giving into the fear that something will happen?"

"It's not the same thing."

She raised an eyebrow. "Why not?"

"It's just protecting what I have. It's a sound financial decision. Nothing more."

"A bodyguard, especially with what's going on is just protecting what you have as well. Isn't that a sound financial decision, too?"

Man, the woman was good. He didn't have a response to that. Not to mention the fact that she was making sense.

"In addition to making a financial mistake, isn't your refusal doing exactly what you were trying to avoid?" Erica shrugged. "The fear is already there. You're letting it prevent you from doing what you need to do. Back then, it was swimming. Now, it's hiring a bodyguard."

Crap. Why had he told her the truth? She was making too much sense for his peace of mind. And he couldn't even fall back on the assurance that she didn't know everything. He'd just told her. Not to mention the fact that he was starting to feel foolish for holding out. Still, the same worry tingled at the back of his mind.

He shouldn't give in.

Erica clasped his hands in hers to get his attention. Once he met her eyes again, she said the magic words. "I'll teach you to swim."

Hope blossomed in his chest, but he quickly extinguished it. Trevor gave her a wry smile when he stood and put some distance between them. That close together, he was sure he'd give her the moon if she'd asked. She almost had.

"You can't teach me to swim. The last person who tried told me I was ruining his life and quit."

Erica rose to the challenge, literally. She stepped toe to toe with him when she said, "Let me be your bodyguard and I will make you a swimmer."

Trevor smirked. She didn't know what she was up against. But if he had a chance to conquer his fear of water, then he knew he could do anything. Though reluctant to admit it, he wanted to try. "Deal."

Erica smiled back. "Deal."

* * * *

Erica was getting fed up. They'd been on the road for the last two weeks and she still hadn't managed to get Trevor in a pool. Four cities and six concerts down and Erica could be having the time of her life. Except she'd promised Trevor she'd teach him to swim and she'd only managed to get him to dip a toe in one pool.

Erica was startled out of her frustration when Megan bustled over and held a checkered fabric swatch under Erica's chin. Trevor's fabulous costumer mumbled under her breath, then grinned.

"Thanks!" She hurried away.

Erica was amazed how fast things had progressed. Like she'd expected, Trevor's band and crew were skeptical at her last minute addition. There'd been plenty of idle speculation on why, but once they saw she had no designs on Trevor, they seemed to lower their protective shields. Once they'd seen her swim, she became one of them.

She was surprised to learn that some of them had pretty colorful backgrounds, but the one thing they all shared was a staunch loyalty to Trevor. He treated them well and with respect, and they tripped over themselves to return the favor.

Having such a loyal staff, both encouraged and frustrated Erica. Encouraged because she knew they could be trusted with his safety. Frustrated because she was able to rule out too many suspects without finding the culprit behind the attacks.

Erica considered Trevor when he headed toward her. He looked ready to leave. Using their predetermined route, they headed to their rental car. Though separate, Trevor was never out of her sight. Since leaving on the tour, Erica would find them both last minute housing apart from his band on the premise that anyone could find them with enough notice.

She'd even stumped his band. Trevor's sudden disappearances after the concerts were apparently newsworthy since he always stuck with them. They laid odds that he had a "sweet little filly," as JimDawg the drummer put it, holed up somewhere that he wasn't ready to share with the rest of them. It amused Erica that they'd made sure she was included in the mornings' bets that the little filly was a blonde, brunette, or redhead. She'd always emerge from her own hotel room late and add her own category. The chick was bald. The guys would crack up and they'd get on with their day.

Her mind snapped back to chew on her current problem. She had to get him in the pool she'd made sure was at their hotel. Before she'd come up with a viable plan, Erica heard Jaclyn declare behind her, "I've told you eight million times, I'm not using your product until you make it easier to take off my performer's faces."

Erica glanced behind her in time to see Trevor's makeup lady slam the cell phone closed and blow out a frustrated breath.

Jaclyn caught Erica's look. "Why is this guy making sales calls at two in the morning anyway? I'm getting a new phone." She tossed up her hands and stalked off. Erica smiled. The woman just helped her figure out how she was going to teach Trevor to swim.

Less than a half an hour later, Erica unpacked the large bowls she'd stopped to buy on their way to the hotel. Trevor studied her with a curious look on his face.

"The pool is beautiful. Wanna go take a dip?"

She was hip to his game. Every time, he'd make her think he was ready to get in the water. Once on the deck, he'd find some pressing excuse to not get in the water. The first pool was too big.

Another too small. A third, too much chlorine. Unfortunately for him, he didn't know that pool didn't use chlorine. Erica recognized the newer facility and realized he'd been stringing her along. She was about to turn the tables on him.

"I don't think we'll have time." Erica went to the small bathroom where she washed and filled the bowls with warm water. She grabbed a couple towels and returned to the main sleeping area with its two double beds.

He looked at his watch. "We have ten whole hours before we're due at the airport."

Erica put the bowls of water on the small table in the corner and sat down. "Jaclyn didn't tell you?" At his blank look, she feigned a resigned look and regarded her bowl. "She's trying some new product, but it seems it's a nightmare to remove."

Trevor sat at the table across from her. Eyed the bowl warily. "She didn't mention anything."

Erica snorted. "Not surprising. I think the sale rep is being a pain. But in the meantime, we're supposed to soak our faces in warm water every night. Just to make sure it's all off."

Trevor scrubbed his knuckles against his cheeks. "Feels pretty clean to me."

Erica shrugged. "Something about the next application looks horrible if you don't get everything off." Though she was dying to watch Trevor to see if he was buying the load of lies she was selling, Erica dipped her face in the bowl of water. She counted to ten then sat up and wiped her face on the towel. Trevor was still staring at her.

She gestured at his bowl. "You just count to ten. Then dry. She said to repeat that ten times."

Erica watched when Trevor moved into position. He eyed the bowl like it was going to attack at any moment. In silence, she cheered him on. She knew he could do this.

When he dipped a finger into the bowl instead of his face, Erica slumped in disappointment. But she wouldn't give up. "I'm so going to look better than you tomorrow night!"

Erica dunked her face again. When she dried it, she found Trevor staring at her with a resigned look in his eyes. "That's a given. But I don't want Jaclyn to look bad. She has enough of a challenge to work with here." He gestured at his gorgeous face before putting it in the bowl.

Erica sucked in a breath. She couldn't help the grin that split her face. He'd just taken a huge step in the right direction. Though she couldn't tell him how proud she was of him because of her lie. Erica was willing to live with that. Once he got comfortable with the bowl, he'd be ready for the pool. She was more than prepared to wait until then.

Chapter Nine

By Erica's estimation, there had to be at least a thousand butterflies attending the hoedown in her belly. She was thankful they didn't begin their party until after she'd swum Trevor's show. Thinking back on their perfect performance brought a smile to Erica's face.

Sadly, it wasn't thoughts of protecting Trevor that was the life of the party in her stomach. The actual case was progressing. Jason had leads to follow left and right. It was the whole teaching him to swim thing. Giving Trevor lessons on the sly, she couldn't know if she was moving too fast or not. She had to trust her instincts. After two more weeks of their daily facials, Erica noticed that he'd become comfortable talking and breathing with his mouth just above the water. It was time to move on to phase two.

Erica selected one of Trecam's safe houses for their stay because it had a pool in the back over which she'd have full control. Trevor didn't know it yet, but he'd uttered his last excuse weeks ago.

Erica marched into his bedroom where Trevor was sitting on the bed clad in only a pair of shorts. One leg dangled over the side while he rested his forearm on a raised knee. Once again, Erica found herself trying not to drool over the sight of his broad chest and muscular arms. His thick blond hair appeared damp, but still curled at his neck. She spared a glance for the laptop between his thighs and continued to his bag that was tossed on a chair.

"What are you doing?" He asked while she rooted through his belongings.

She grinned triumphantly and pulled out his swim trunks. Waving them in the air, she stalked toward him. "There's a pool out back. Let's go."

"I showered a while ago."

"So you can shower again. Move it."

"Will you be in it?" He quirked an eyebrow, but she could see in his eyes that his mind was elsewhere. Erica figured he was too worried about the upcoming lesson to put his usual panache behind the flirtation. She decided to shock him.

"What if I say yes?"

Trevor's eyebrows disappeared up under his damp locks. The hope disappeared from his expression when he frowned at her. "What's the catch?"

She tossed the swim trunks at him and headed for the door. Erica added a little extra sway to her hips and looked at him over her shoulder. "You'll have to swim to find out." With that, she pulled the door closed behind her so he could dress—or not. Although, she hoped he would. He had no idea how far he'd come, and she wanted to show him.

* * * *

There were a million and one reasons Trevor shouldn't follow Erica out to the pool. But most damning was the latest obstacle he'd just learned was between them.

When they'd pulled up outside, the address tickled in his subconscious, but he'd ignored it. As had become his custom, he'd teased her and made suggestive remarks until she'd headed back to the hotel to make her late night reappearance for the band's sake.

While she'd been gone, he couldn't get the address out of his head. He'd logged on to his portfolio and discovered the worst. The address was on a list of holdings he'd purchased. Those purchases made their way through shell corporations until they'd reached the assets of Trecam. This was one of their safe houses.

There was no way Erica would have access to it unless she worked for Trecam and, thus, for him.

Trevor stood and fiddled with the trunks she'd tossed at him. He knew he should confront her with what he'd learned, except everything inside of him screamed that it would change their relationship in a fundamental way. He'd worked too hard to get them to this point, and he wasn't about to undo it all. He'd tell her once he was more confident of where he stood with her.

Although he had always teased her that he just had seduction in mind, nothing could be further from the truth. He was beginning to see Erica having a more permanent place in his life. He'd been careful to keep her in the dark, but he'd kept tabs on how the band and crew reacted to her. She'd gotten overwhelmingly favorable reviews. It amused him to think how they'd all made a point of including her in the pool regarding his whereabouts the previous night even though they knew good and well he was with her. They didn't know the bodyguard part, and Trevor was in no hurry to let them in on that little tidbit. Still, it meant a lot to him that his band approved.

It had been Trevor's plan to woo her for real once she'd caught his tormentor. A truck sized wrench had been thrown into that plan when he learned she worked for Trecam. He couldn't ask her to give up working for the most prestigious agency in the world. Which is what he'd have to do if they ever expected to see each other. He would give up the rock star thing in a hot second, but he couldn't continue to fund Trecam if he did. That wasn't an option because their causes were too worthy — too just. They'd caught the occasional stinker, but overall, they were making a difference. And they needed his money to do it.

Trevor heaved a heavy sigh. No way could he work through this tonight. He considered the trunks he had gripped in his hand. The last thing he wanted to do was suffer through a swim lesson. Just because she'd left, didn't mean she'd given up. He was surprised to have put her off this long. With excuses already tumbling around in his brain, Trevor shucked his shorts in favor of the trunks and headed out to the pool.

* * * *

Erica crossed from one side of the pool to the other with her strong eggbeater. She alternated between holding each arm up and both and watched the door for Trevor's appearance. She smiled when he showed at last. She whip kicked to the shallow end.

"Come on in. The water's amazing," she invited when she sat on the stairs.

He eyed her for a long moment. Erica held her breath. He had to make the decision. She couldn't just push him in. Not if she expected to keep the progress they had made. After a long while, he stepped from the deck and into the water. His brows shot up in apparent surprise.

"It's warm."

"I know. Isn't it great?" She patted the stair beside her. "Have a sit down."

Erica watched with bated breath when he hesitated. Trevor eased his tall frame down until he was sitting next to her. He looked at her seeming somewhat amazed.

"It's not that bad."

Confident she had him right where she wanted him, Erica leaned back in the water. "I heard tomorrow's show has been sold out for weeks," she commented. She fought a satisfied smile when she saw Trevor recline in the water, too.

"The rumored scalped price is seventy-five percent higher than what we charge. I'm thinking about sending out my own scalpers. That way the people who are working could at least benefit."

Trevor and Erica sat there on the stairs discussing everything under the sun for over an hour. Not once did Trevor complain. Nor did he get out. Erica smiled to herself. Phase two was complete. Although, something about his demeanor still nagged at her. She remembered her insinuation to convince him to come out and realized that not once had he mentioned it. He hadn't even made any of his other innuendos either. Erica decided to put it down to his overcoming his fear of water. Pride in him made a smile burst forth on her lips.

"What's got you looking like a Cheshire cat over there?"

She hadn't planned to tell him about her fib, but she couldn't hold back her glee. Besides, she wanted him to celebrate, too. It was his milestone.

"Do you realize how long you've been sitting here?"

Trevor shrugged. "Yeah. So?"

"You're progressing very nicely with your swim lessons."

He looked at her like she'd just sprouted a third eyeball. "Lessons? We never even began any lessons." He turned his nose up. "I have half a mind to demand my money back."

Erica laughed at him. "I've been giving you lessons since we left." He still looked blank. She challenged, "Dip your face in the water."

He frowned and looked at the water for such a long time that Erica began to think her celebration may have been a tad premature. Then Trevor complied. He sat up and wiped the water from his eyes with a calm hand. Erica clapped with glee.

"What's the big deal? It's no different that Jaclyn's bowls."

"Exactly."

Erica watched the light dawn in Trevor's eyes.

"There was never any 'new makeup' was there?"

Erica shook her head. "Sorry I had to trick you, but you kept fighting me. And look at your progress. You're more than halfway to knowing how to swim outright!"

Trevor eyed her, hope shining in his eyes. He dipped his face in the water again. Longer, this time. After a long moment, he sat up with a huge grin on his face. "What's next, Teach?"

Erica shook her head. "Class is over for the day. We'll pick up here, tomorrow." They shared a smile. But it was one she hadn't seen on Trevor before. She didn't know what it meant. Or if it meant anything at all.

"What is it?"

He leered up at her. "Just enjoying the view." Erica didn't buy it for a second. Before she could question him, he stood to go inside. "G'night."

Erica caught up to him by the patio door. "Trevor? Is there something I should know?"

He affected a blank look, and she could tell it cost him. Something was definitely going on. "Not a thing."

"If anything else has happened, you need to tell me."

He lifted a finger and traced a drop of water along her collar bone. Like he'd just realized what he was doing, he jerked his hand away. The rock star smile surfaced. "Just a personal epiphany."

She knew he was telling her as much truth as he was going

to. "Good night, then."

"G'night." Trevor ducked inside. And she let him.

* * * *

Trevor was hell on wheels the next day. Erica fought to hold on to her own temper while he sent the band and her through all sorts of needless changes. But what puzzled her most were the sympathetic looks she was getting from everyone. From the band, the crew, the backup singers and dancers. When they were nearing show time, Erica began to put two and two together. Her worst suspicions were confirmed when Megan shooed everyone out while she fitted Erica. The woman had done a marvelous job recreating the suit demolished during the yacht crash, and Erica learned in short order that in addition to being a fabulous seamstress, she also considered herself to be mama hen. Very funny since she was the youngest on the crew.

"I used a softer material around the seams. How's it feel?" Erica twisted from side to side and smiled when nothing chaffed.

"Perfect. Trevor is lucky to have you."

Megan shot a knowing look at Erica in the full length mirror. "I think he's lucky to have you." The woman returned some straight pins to her bulging pin cushion so she could speak more clearly. "Just you hang in. Whatever bug he got up his butt will die soon enough."

Erica looked at the woman with a puzzled frown. "Wait. You think I had something to do with it?"

Megan cocked her head to the side and smiled. "It's just a little lover's quarrel. Trust me. You'll get through it."

Erica put her hands up and shook her head. "Lover's . . . no. Where on earth did you get that idea? I'm just like you. Part of the staff."

"C'mon Erica, we're not stupid. Everybody knows he goes wherever he goes at night with you." Megan pulled another costume from the rack and made some adjustments.

Erica was stunned to her core. She tried to laugh it off. "Whatever. I'm at the hotel with you guys every night. What Trevor does is his business."

Megan put down her work to give Erica her full attention. "We all like you. That means you're family. We'll play along with your lies — for a while. Then you might want to try something new."

"My lies?"

"You don't have to worry about your reputation. We all know Trevor would never get involved with a woman unless he was serious. That and his incessant asking what we think of you. That's why I can tell you without a doubt that this spat, whatever it is, will blow over."

Erica was so furious all she could see was red. She'd been killing herself to keep her cover alive where the band was concerned. To find out that he'd casually told them everything snapped the camel's back in two. Although it appears he left out a detail or two, Erica seethed. She wondered what Megan would say if she told her the whole truth. Erica shook off her vindictive streak. She had to come up with plan B. And maybe find a silver lining to this little development.

"It's not a lover's spat. He was fine one moment, the next. . ." She gestured to where Trevor issued a well-timed bellow. "I can't figure it."

"That is odd, indeed. I've only seen him act like this one other time. It was when it looked like he wasn't going to get something he wanted."

Erica frowned and glanced at the closed door. "And what happened?"

Megan shrugged. "He got it."

Lindsay, the stage manager tapped on the door before sticking her head in. "Five minutes to curtain, Megs. Who do you need?"

While Megan ran over the list of people on whom she needed to make last minute adjustments, Erica replayed the previous night's events in her head. What had changed? He'd said it was personal. So it couldn't have anything to do with her. He'd known all along that he couldn't have her. But that hadn't stopped him from chipping away at her resistance anyway. She remembered his sudden backing off. Had something happened to make him realize that his efforts were fruitless?

"Knock 'em dead!" Megan told her then pushed Erica out of the dressing room to make room for those coming in.

Erica stood against the wall for a long moment considering. Her more charitable half that wanted to give Trevor the benefit of the doubt was scorched away by the half that was white hot anger. How dare he jeopardize his life so carelessly when she was busting her butt to save it? With her fury rolling off her in waves, she went to find Trevor. They needed to work this out now.

She reached the edge of the stage just when the auditorium went totally black. She could feel the rush of audience anticipation when a lone white light swept over them. At length, it blasted full power on the stage where Trevor stood wearing his rock star smile.

The crowd went wild. Trevor was eating it up. The man was born to perform. The tense lines that framed his eyes all day began to ease when he launched into the first number. Seeing him having a blast when she was so furious with him just made Erica that much angrier.

Before she could think of a suitable punishment, Lindsay took her arm. "In the tank you go, Eri."

Even the nickname Lindsay insisted on calling her irritated Erica. She took a breath and tried to remind herself that the girl had nicknames for everyone. She gave the stage manager a brittle smile and headed off to slide in the water for her performance. Being in the water meant she wouldn't be able to catch Trevor when he came offstage for his wardrobe change either. But she had a job to do. She let Lindsay push her away.

Erica just went through the motions during the beginning of the routine. She still performed with excellence, but her heart just wasn't in it. She missed her timing on a hybrid and had to improvise to get back on track. This was all Trevor's fault. No fair he was having the show of his life while she was struggling to even concentrate on what she did best.

Erica swam under the stage for her appearance on Trevor's left. He was standing where he always stood singing his heart out and grinning at her when she surfaced for a jump. Erica couldn't take anymore. She did some quick calculations in her mind and rewrote this section of the routine. Instead of spinning quietly down, she did quick twists and splatted a leg down on every rotation. She sprayed Trevor with each splat. She longed to see his face, but she settled for hearing his voice falter through the underwater speakers.

This time, when she surfaced, a huge smile was on her face.

She quirked an eyebrow at Trevor and she saw the answering anger spring in his eyes. Erica swirled so her back was to him and did a surface boost. When she came back down, she arched her back to send another spray of water Trevor's way.

She grudgingly gave him credit. He kept singing just like he'd arranged for this shower in the middle of the show. Still, he had nowhere to go. Only a shallow, narrow bulkhead that doubled as a stage running through the middle of the pool. Erica's domain. When he hugged the edge opposite of where Erica was, she swam under the stage and surfaced. When she came up, she took a mouthful of water and sprayed his chest with a graceful arch of the liquid. All Trevor could do was glare at her. She smiled and continued to swim, splashing him every chance she got. By the end of the number, Trevor was just standing there and taking the punishment.

Erica ended the number in the usual fashion by swimming up the tower at the back of the stage. She struck her normal pose and the lights went out. Much calmer, Erica continued the swim to the top for her portable oxygen tank before diving back to the bottom and out. When she came back down, she saw Trevor was waiting for her to get out. She turned right side up and faced him through the glass.

He crooked a finger signaling for her to come to him. Erica lifted an eyebrow and folded her arms in challenge. She mouthed, "I'm right here." She signaled for him to come to her.

Trevor's glower got even darker if it were possible. He puffed out his cheeks then folded his arms like he was going to settle in and wait for her to run out of air.

Erica smirked and took a puff from the oxygen tank. She shrugged. "What?"

She could tell he was on the verge of stamping his foot when Megan caught him by his arm and thrust a towel at him. She pulled him away to get changed and threw an amused smile and a wink over her shoulder at Erica where she was still floating in the tank.

Erica made it a point to be in the tank every time Trevor came offstage. For the finale, Erica swam the routine like it was written. She noticed Trevor flinched when she first swam out. But while the number progressed, they'd become a solid team again.

Although, she was still pretty mad at him for talking to the crew. And she could tell all wasn't forgiven on his side either. They were in for a fun conversation later.

Not willing to put it off any longer, Erica made her way out of the tank and waited for Trevor to come offstage. Like she'd figured, he attacked first.

"What was that?"

"You wanna have this out here or in semi-private?" she asked. She inclined her head, indicating the crew breaking down the stage and pretending not to listen around them.

Trevor grabbed her arm and led her to a corner that was secluded for the time being.

"You wanna tell me what's going on with you?"

"Why don't we start with what's going on with you?" Erica countered. "You've been snarling at everybody all day."

"I haven't."

"Kara was almost in tears and JimDawg had to pull a punch. What's wrong with you?"

"Wait a minute. You didn't stop him did you?"

"It's not in my job description to stop people who love you from reacting when you're being an ass! You owe them an apology."

"An ass? That's rich. Coming from the chick who just spit on the star onstage." He stepped closer, like he thought he could intimidate her with his height.

Erica leaned in to whisper angrily, "The way you were running your mouth about our supposed hot and heavy romance, I thought you could use a little cooling off."

"Running my mouth? I haven't . . ."

"Save it, Trevor. I didn't think I could be more clear. All anyone was supposed to know was that I'm a good swimmer." She poked him hard in the chest. "Imagine my surprise when your current mood is blamed on me and our lovers' spat." She poked him again. He caught her hand stopping her from doing any more damage to his torso.

"I just wanted to know what they thought of you and if you fit in." Trevor softened his stare. "Is that so wrong?"

"When it interferes in my keeping you alive, yes!" Erica blew out a breath of anger. "You can't go and change my cover behind my back. What if the guy we're looking for was one of them?"

Trevor jerked away from her. "He's not."

"What if he were? Do you understand what kind of danger you just put me in? If the person figured you and I were close, they'd be smart to use me to get to you. Then I'm out of commission and can no longer protect you. Did you even bother to think of that?"

"That would never happen," Trevor protested, but Erica could see that he was giving her words some serious weight.

"It happens . . ." Erica's breath whooshed out of her like someone opened a valve and let all the air escape. Trevor frowned and took her hand. She squeezed it in a painful grip.

"What's wrong?"

* * * *

"They said you were back here," a super sweet voice said from behind him. Still, with all that syrup, Trevor could hear the sharp edge of bitterness running through it. He turned around to see three women heading toward them. The one in the middle seemed to be leading the way followed by a younger lady on each side. All three wore press passes from the local media.

It took him a moment, but he recognized Dani, Erica's old duet partner. Time had not been kind to the woman. She couldn't have been much older than Erica, yet she looked like she had at least a decade on her. He eyed their passes, but there were no recorders, no cameras, no notebooks, no other sign that they were there on professional business. He was positive Erica hadn't invited her to watch the show. Even if he didn't know Erica better than that, the way she was clinging to his hand told him just how surprised she was to see her.

Trevor turned on his rock star smile until he could figure out what was going on. "Ladies. Did you enjoy the show?"

The young one to Dani's right hurried forward and gushed, "It was amazing! I loved watching you swim. I wish I could do that hybrid you did toward the end of the second number. It was wonderful."

Erica gathered her wits enough to smile a little and say, "Thank you."

Dani pulled the girl back, and their third comrade glared at her. She looked cowed enough and turned her attention to the floor. Dani leveled a narrow look at Erica.

"Back in the pool, I see." She looked up at the impressive tank Trevor had built for her. "Sort of."

"Dani. How are you?" Trevor had never heard Erica so quiet and timid. What he would give to know what had gone down between these two at the Olympics.

The third woman piped up. "She's been amazing. She led our team to the National Championship last year. I don't expect we'll have any trouble defending our title this year." She looked at Dani, her case of hero worship clear in her eyes. "I've never seen a swimmer as good as Dani."

Erica flinched when the woman's intended barb that even though they'd seen the show she still hadn't seen a swimmer as good hit home. He was decidedly sick of them.

"Dani is very good," the woman continued.

"But you. You just have raw nerve. I can't believe you'd actually wear the costume I made for you to try to make your pathetic little comeback." Dani got in Erica's face. Trevor's heart ached when Erica backed away. "What? Do you finally regret not wearing it in the Games? Or were you upset to learn that you hadn't destroyed me like you intended so you went for public embarrassment?"

"I didn't try to destroy you. I just . . ."

"Save it, Erica. Your little diva episode is well-documented."

"I'm sorry, Dani. I don't know what else to tell you." Erica stopped cowering. "It looks like you've done well for yourself. National champion and all. You're still swimming. Isn't that what it's about?"

Erica never saw it coming. Or if she did, she didn't bother to move when Dani swung.

Chapter Ten

Trevor flinched when Dani's open palm connected with Erica's cheek. Erica just stood there looking like she was somewhere between stunned and believing she deserved it. When the woman swung again, Trevor grabbed her hand in a pain inducing grasp before it could connect with Erica's face.

Pandemonium broke out when the crew beat security over to protect one of their own. Megan and Lindsay pulled Erica back, and JimDawg helped Trevor restrain Dani. The women with her just stared at everybody in shock.

"Get her out of here!" Trevor bellowed when the security guards arrived to subdue the woman.

"I'm so sorry, Dani. I'm so sorry," Erica repeated.

"Stop apologizing to her," Trevor ordered. He nailed Dani with a harsh look. "I'm going to press charges."

Dani's eyes widened indicating that the seriousness of her actions penetrated her head. She went on the offensive. "It was self-defense."

Erica broke free of Megan and Lindsay. "Trevor, just let it go," she pleaded with him. Erica squeezed his shoulder. "Let it go."

Dani's anger rekindled when Erica went to bat for her. "I

want my crystals back, too." She ripped free of the guard's grip and yanked the crystals from Erica's costume tearing the suit in the process. Trevor stepped between the women again, stopping the onslaught when Erica couldn't pull away from Dani's grasp.

"Take her now!" The security guards dragged a screaming Dani away. Trevor shrugged out of his shirt and wrapped it around Erica since the suit was almost in shreds. He handed her over to Megan.

Erica looked at the other woman with tears in her eyes. "I'm so sorry about your costume."

"Nonsense. It was pretty amateurish anyway." She looked over her shoulder at Trevor. "I'll have her ready to go in about ten minutes."

Trevor nodded and watched Lindsay and Megan escort Erica away. JimDawg clapped Trevor on the shoulder. "What was that about?"

He shrugged. "Erica says I owe you an apology." Trevor looked at JimDawg. "I'm sorry I was an idiot all day."

JimDawg smiled. "You're in new territory, my man. When JamieDee and I first got together she could throw me in a pretty good spin, too. It'll pass."

Trevor smiled and chose not to correct him like he knew Erica would have insisted. Hey, he apologized. She'd gotten one of two. She'd have to be content with that. He thought about what had just happened. He needed to find out what went down at the Olympics. Without the information, he was afraid he wouldn't be able to protect her. In light of their role reversal, he hoped she wouldn't be as stubborn as he had been.

* * * *

Erica hurried to dress and left the remains of her costume with Megan who promised to have a new one for her by the time they arrived at their next stop. Erica thanked her and rushed out to find Trevor. She had to get him back to the safe house. No matter how much of a loop she'd been thrown for, she still had a job to do.

She was grateful when she saw Trevor waiting for her. She got him in their car and zoomed back to the safe house. She tried to put off all the questions she figured he had by keeping a steady stream of chatter flowing. She decided to skip her normal nightly swim in favor of a hot shower and bed.

Once she stepped under the spray, all the emotions she'd tried to keep at bay rushed over her. Even though Erica had been the darling of their duet, Dani had the bigger mouth. Erica was always the more no nonsense hard worker while Dani took the time to chat people up at practice. The result had been that when things went down, people just believed what they'd been told. Not being a big talker, Erica hadn't been surprised when they'd taken her silence for an admission of guilt. Seeing how mad Dani still was, there was no way their mutual acquaintances hadn't taken Dani's side. With self-pity weighing her down, Erica shut off the water and got out of the shower.

* * * *

Trevor knew the exact moment Erica entered her bedroom. The sweet scent of her shampoo heralded her arrival better than any fanfare ever could. He opened one eye in time to see the surprise on her face when she found him lounging on her bed. Still rubbing her hair dry, Erica crept in and looked around.

"Wanna tell me what happened between you and Dani?"

Erica tore her gaze from her bag in the corner and stared at him. Trevor crossed his long legs making himself comfortable.

"No." She gave him a defiant look.

Trevor quirked an eyebrow when she turned off the light and climbed into the bed. He turned on the lamp on his side table. "I think you owe me an explanation."

Erica pulled the pillow over her head. "I can't help what you think."

Trevor regarded her for a long moment. He turned out the light and stretched out beside her. "Does this help? Something revealed in the dark won't seem quite as bad."

"Don't do this, Trevor," she pleaded.

"Don't do what? Care about you? Whatever you're holding back is eating you alive. You almost went catatonic when you saw Dani."

"Can't we just forget about her?"

"I can. But can you?" Trevor waited for Erica's response. When none came he rolled over and gathered her in his arms. "What really happened, Erica? I know you too well to believe you became a diva all of a sudden."

Erica sucked in a breath. "You looked it up? How long've you known?"

"Since before we left."

* * * *

Erica took a moment to let that sink in. All this time he had to have been wondering. And then tonight . . . tonight was her every nightmare come true. She remembered how Trevor hadn't hesitated to jump into the fray for her. Maybe she did owe him an explanation.

"It was a bomb." She heard Trevor's sharp intake of breath at her quiet admission.

"I stumbled upon it just before we were supposed to swim. Interpol diffused it, but it took too long. I'd missed the competitions." Erica tried to shrug it off like she didn't care. She'd done the right thing, but that didn't stave off her own bitter disappointment. She'd missed the opportunity to swim in the Olympics. Dani wasn't the only one hurt by the incident. To have gotten so close just to have it ripped away.

Like she'd expected, Trevor wasn't about to let her off that easy. Along with the friendship that had developed between them, she knew he also could read her the same way she could him. She didn't need him to say anything to confirm that he knew she'd left a whole lot out.

* * * *

"When you say stumbled upon it, what does that mean exactly?"

Erica sighed and remained silent for so long that Trevor started to think she wasn't going to answer him. But he knew she just needed a moment. He was going to give it to her. "Dani wanted a fourth nose clip. Since I was going to the bathroom anyway, I offered to get it for her. The floor was wet. When I opened her locker, I slipped. I caught myself on this thing that had all kinds of wires sticking out and a timer started counting down."

Trevor felt her tremble at the memory. He could relate. He tightened his embrace around her, trying to reassure her that she was safe.

"They had given us these little panic buttons. I was too scared to move anything else, but my thumb sure got a workout. Security came to check on me. One happened to be with Interpol. He concocted the story that I was having a diva episode and cleared the locker room. They didn't want to start a panic while they diffused it.

"Four hours later, I was free. But my entire team, especially Dani, hated me—correction—hate me. Judging by tonight, they all still do." Trevor's heart was breaking at the pain he heard in Erica's voice. He decided to put the blame right where it belonged.

"Wait a minute, you found a bomb in Dani's bag. And Dani hates you? Did you put it there?"

Erica snorted. "I might as well have. She was dating this loser. I always encouraged her to cut him loose. Right before we left for the games, she did.

"During those four long hours, I made friends with the Interpol guys. When the evidence started pointing back toward synchro people, they asked for my perspective. I helped them learn it was loser boyfriend who'd tried to kill Dani."

Trevor stroked her hair. "What an ungrateful . . ."

"She has no idea, Trevor." Erica shrugged. "I can't blame her for something she doesn't know."

Trevor's arms tightened around her again. "I can." He leaned over to kiss her temple then sat up preparing to leave.

"Trevor." Erica looked at him. Indecisiveness all over her face. Even in the darkened room Trevor could see her vulnerable expression. He wasn't used to that. "Thanks."

He nodded, still watching her. He could feel that wasn't all. She dropped his gaze. Not like her, either, he thought. Then she shocked him to his core.

"Stay." He had to strain to hear her quiet whisper. Still, he was sure he'd misunderstood. "I mean. If you think you can behave yourself."

His heart swelled at the notion that she might be letting him in at last. "I think that can be arranged." He kicked off his shoes and climbed back into the bed next to her. This was an extraordinarily bad idea. But he wasn't about to toss back the bone she'd offered him. He wrapped his arms around her and held on until she drifted off to sleep. Trevor was thankful that the next day was a travel day because he knew he wasn't going to be getting much sleep that night.

Trevor was startled awake the next morning when something smacked across him. He stretched and pried one eye open.

"Morning, sunshine!" Erica, all dressed, was standing over him with a towel dangling from her hand.

"It's too early for this," he complained and rolled over.

"You don't even know what time it is." She snapped his backside with the towel and opened the curtains. Sunlight streamed in.

Trevor rolled to his back and followed her movements when she headed back toward the door. He noticed that her bags were packed.

"I'll bite. What time is it?" He sat up a little and rubbed his eyes. He was surprised to note that he was well rested. And far too comfy to get up.

"Time for you to hit the shower if you don't want to miss the second flight."

"Second flight? What happened to the first one?"

"We kinda slept through it." She snapped him again with the towel. "Get moving. I wanna strip the bed."

Trevor let her propel him to the bathroom. He grimaced when he noted his wrinkled clothes. He looked at her. "Want any help? I can get my room."

"I got those first. But thanks for offering." He nodded and headed to the bathroom.

* * * *

Glad he was gone, Erica sat on the edge of the bed. She was relieved he hadn't brought up her embarrassing meltdown the night before. Then again, she hadn't exactly given him time. Erica pushed herself up to get the sheets off the bed and remake it with fresh ones. Since this was a safe house they didn't have the luxury of maid service.

Erica wasn't upset that they'd missed their first flight. Most of the band would've been aboard. She wasn't sure she was ready to face any of them just yet. Of course now it wouldn't matter how much she protested that she and Trevor weren't together. This latest lapse would do nothing but confirm what they already believed they knew.

Erica reflected on how sweet Trevor was about the whole Dani thing and figured that there were worse things to be known as than Trevor Cole's girlfriend. Before he'd even known the whole story, he'd jumped in on her behalf. She was very grateful. Especially after the hard time she'd given him during the show. She should apologize for her behavior. That he'd been so understanding and supportive just made her feel that much guiltier.

She couldn't believe she'd told him about the bomb. She'd never told anybody about it. In part because Interpol had warned her not to, but for the most part because she didn't think anyone would believe her. Not only had Trevor believed her, but he'd made Dani out to be the bad guy in the situation. Erica's sure hands slowed in tucking the sheets around the mattress when she began to see things from Trevor's perspective. She saved Dani's life. Erica had nothing to apologize for.

Trevor appeared in the doorway. He still had a towel slung low around his hips, and his boxers dangled from his fingers. "Though I appreciate it, laying out my clothes is not in your job description."

Erica smiled at his affronted tone. "No. But getting you where you need to be on time is. Packing your things was the best way to do that." She bundled the sheets up in her arms. He stepped back to let her out of the room. She stopped next to him while a ridiculous idea went through her head. She couldn't do it. She shouldn't anyway.

But she did. Erica stood on her tiptoes and gave Trevor a quick peck on his lips. His eyebrows shot up in surprise.

"Thank you."

Before he could gather his wits or she could get in anymore trouble, Erica fled for the laundry room.

* * * *

Trevor stood there with a dumb smile on his face. He was making progress. His thoughts went back to his funding her agency thing, but all of a sudden that obstacle no longer seemed insurmountable. He could be a patient guy. His cell phone rang, dragging him out of his pleased reverie.

Erica was busy folding sheets and putting them back in the linen closet when Trevor shuffled in. She glanced at him, and frowned. She took a quick look at her watch.

"Gotta go, gotta go."

"Change of plans," he informed her and held up his cell phone. "Apparently, a water pipe burst in the venue, and it's flooded. Might not be a big deal for you, but the rest of landlubbers decided a vacation was in order."

Erica closed the closet door to give him her full attention. He could see the wheels turning in her head and held up a hand. He was quick to reassure her that his attacker wasn't responsible. "As much as I'd like everything to be about me, this one isn't. The pipes weren't in that great a shape when we were there last time — four years ago."

Erica nodded and relaxed her tense posture. "Then home before the next stop? I'd like . . ."

"Actually, I was hoping to see my parents during the break. We're close enough to drive from here, and it's just for a few days."

* * * *

His parents? Erica didn't like the sound of this. In fact, she hated it. Did he expect her to be his girlfriend there, too? She was positive she didn't want to endure the 'how many kids' or 'where will you live' questions on a real level much less a fake one.

"And where would we stay while at your parents?"

"On the ranch, of course. They have plenty of room."

"In this plenty of room, I'm supposed to pretend to be your girlfriend or can we tell them I'm your bodyguard?"

"They'd believe the girlfriend thing a whole lot easier." He frowned. "I think."

"Are you seeing the problems I see with this scenario?" She squeezed his arm. "I don't see how we can make it work." She pressed by him into the living room.

"I already told my mom we were coming."

"Call her back. Tell her something came up."

"You don't know my mother. If we cancel now, she'll join us on tour."

Seeing Trevor's panic at the prospect, Erica pinched the bridge of her nose. She hoped she wouldn't regret this. "Give me the layout of the house and land. I'll work out security."

"You really think that's necessary?" At the look Erica gave him, he reached for a pencil and notepad. "Alrighty then."

* * * *

Erica's stomach clenched with anxiety. According to the GPS in the rental car she drove, she was just fourteen minutes from meeting Trevor's family—as his girlfriend no less. Under other circumstances, Erica would have been excited. But because she knew it was all a lie, she just hoped she could endure fifty two hours of constant scrutiny and keep her cover intact.

She grilled Trevor about how much his relatives knew about the attacks. He assured her that he hadn't given them details. Still, he was a celebrity. There was no way they hadn't gotten more than he'd imagined from the media. Erica took a breath. It would be okay. Just a few of Trevor's closest relatives. She could handle a few of Trevor's immediate family members. It wouldn't even be his whole immediate family. She'd just lay low and ride it out.

The GPS announced that Erica was to turn left. Erica followed the instruction and slammed on the brakes. She smacked Trevor with the back of her hand startling him from his nap. He sat up and blinked.

"Wha . . . what's happening?"

"That's what I'd like to know." She gestured to the cars lining both sides of the narrow road. In this isolated part of the country, all these people could have just one destination—theirs.

Chapter Eleven

"Tell me this isn't your house," Erica pleaded. "I made a wrong turn somewhere, didn't I?"

Trevor looked around and groaned. "You didn't make a mistake. The actual driveway is just ahead on the left."

"Trevor, this isn't . . . I can't protect you from all these people."

Hearing the uncertainty in her voice he patted her hand where it rested on the gearshift. "You won't have to. He's not going to be here. And if he is, he'll stick out like a sore thumb."

She looked at him. "How do you figure that?"

"Small community. I recognize most of these vehicles. Everybody'll know everybody else." He gave her a smile. "I'm afraid you'll be the most suspicious one here."

"Not funny, Trevor. Did you ever think that he's someone you know?"

Trevor looked back at the road while he seemed to consider that notion for the first time. He turned his attention back to her. "You'll just have to stick close, then, won't you?" He squeezed her hand. "That won't be so bad will it?"

His eyes drilled into hers. She knew he was asking about

more than just her job. She couldn't answer that question. Her job wouldn't let her give him the answer she knew he wanted. She decided to answer the question most relevant at the moment.

"It's going to be horrible. Trying to ascertain ulterior motives of a hundred people by the looks of it is going to be miserable." She checked out the cars along the road. She couldn't meet his stare when she added, almost against her will, "I'll adjust, though." From the corner of her eye, she saw Trevor smile. He kept a hold on her hand when he pointed out the driveway.

Erica eased them forward again. Her greatest fears were confirmed when the long driveway was also lined with cars. When they approached the house, she spotted a huge tent in the back. Her estimate of only one hundred shot up. Erica gritted her teeth while she eased the car toward the house. Not caring who she double parked, she turned their car around so it was headed back the way they'd come. Just in case they needed a quick getaway. Trevor gave her hand one final pat then climbed from the car.

His appearance was met by excited squeals. Then he was enveloped in hugs and surrounded with chatter before Erica could even emerge from behind the wheel. She was going to have to talk to him about that. Seeing his excited face while he greeted old friends and family, she knew it would have to wait.

Erica was stunned to hear her own name called. She turned around to see Cam wheeling his way toward her. Her confusion must have been evident on her face because he greeted her with apologies.

"I'm so sorry about all this. Marcy was talking to my mother on the phone when Trevor's mother called her to go shopping for Trevor's Welcome Home feast. Of course my mother told Marcy why she had to get off the phone. Marcy invited us herself. And on this end, my mom and Abby can't ever do anything quietly. Before they'd gotten out of the store, the whole town had been invited to 'stop by' and none of this would've ever happened if my wife hated her in-laws like she's supposed to."

Erica's surprise melted into amusement at Cam's rambling explanation. Erica squeezed his shoulder in sympathy. "Got it." She looked around the crowd again. Cam noted her uncertainty.

"And I figured you could use a little back up."

Erica met his gaze again and nodded. "I never would've let

him come if I'd known . . ."

"You couldn't have stopped him." They turned to watch Trevor greeting the partygoers. Erica was surprised to see that he had an eye on her and Cam. "We got here first."

Erica raised an eyebrow. Cam grimaced.

"A siren and lights are pretty handy at times." She laughed, and then he continued, "I've personally seen everyone who's arrived. No strangers."

"And . . ."

Cam anticipated her question. "And no one with old grudges, either. At least that I know of."

Erica nodded and found Trevor had appeared by her side all of a sudden.

"Don't you have a woman, old man? Always trying to take mine."

Cam grinned. "Like I ever have to try." He glanced at Erica, concern all over his face.

"New cover," she whispered. Cam nodded, and she went back to scanning the crowd.

* * * *

In the midst of greeting the partygoers, Trevor knew Cam's eyes stayed on the possessive arm he'd slung around Erica's waist. He met his friend's eyes behind Erica's back and knew he'd figured that he was doing his darndest to turn the cover real. Cam shook his head in warning, but Trevor shrugged it off. Knowing Cam, he'd corner him soon enough for one of his little talks. In the meantime, he was going to enjoy himself and enjoy having Erica here with him.

Mind made up, he let the crowd suck him and Erica into their midst. While they moved around the side of the house to the main action he casually linked their fingers.

Trevor scanned the familiar faces for his mother. In all his years, he'd never brought a girl home before. He was curious to see what her reaction to Erica would be. He would have no trouble keeping this so called "cover" going. He brought their linked fingers up to his lips for a quick kiss.

He could get used to having her by his side. In fact, he was afraid he already was. When Erica shot him a subtle glare, he knew he should back off a little.

Trevor was thrown off balance when a body launched itself at him. Arms wrapped around his neck, legs around his waist and lips landed squarely on his. His gaze shot to Erica's. She was prepped to use her free hand to disengage the kisser when he swung her out of Erica's grasp. There was just one person would have the gumption to greet him like this and he didn't want Erica to make a spectacle of herself. Trevor pried the arms from around his neck and pulled back to look at his attacker.

"Doggonit, Trisha Loo. You trying to put me in the dog house?" Trevor asked the girl with a grin.

"Don't worry. I'll come visit." She fluttered her lashes at him.

"Trisha, this is Erica. Erica, Trisha Loo. She's a little enthusiastic."

Trisha Loo had the nerve to balance herself on his hip while reaching over to shake Erica's hand. She looked back at Trevor, dismissing Erica.

"So, Trev, where've ya been keeping yourself?"

Trevor was surprised when Erica answered for him. "We've been on tour." He found himself liking the jealous glint he'd caught a glimpse of in Erica's eye.

"Wouldn't you be more comfortable standing?" Trevor asked. Once upon a time, he'd have enjoyed her position. Especially when she wriggled her hips like she was doing now.

"I don't know. I'm pretty comfortable where I am."

Erica put a deceptive but gentle hand on Trisha Loo's shoulder. All of a sudden, her grasp on him went slack. Trevor had to guide her so she wouldn't collapse in a heap at his feet. He needn't have worried. Erica smiled and patted the other woman's shoulder stopping whatever she'd done. "Isn't that better?"

Trisha Loo glared daggers up at Erica even though she was a good six inches shorter. Trevor quickly slid behind Erica and wrapped his arms around her waist to keep Trisha Loo off of him.

"Good to see you, Trish. You know where my mom is? I can't wait for her to meet Erica."

Trisha Loo tore her eyes from Erica's and smiled at Trevor. "She's in the kitchen." With an incredible boldness, she trailed her fingers down Trevor's arm beneath Erica's. "See you later, Trevor," she crooned and sauntered off.

Enjoying the embrace, Trevor was reluctant to let go of Erica. All too soon, he did and was surprised when she turned around and stepped close. She draped her arms over his shoulders and smiled up at him. He would've enjoyed the progress except her eyes were deadly serious.

"I can't protect you here. What if she'd had a needle and stuck you in the neck." Erica's fingers played with his neck. Before Trevor could lose himself in her touch, she continued, "Right here and you'd just be paralyzed. But here"—she moved her fingers a fraction, sending even more electricity up and down his spine—"you'd be dead in an instant."

"I've known all these people my whole life. They've had plenty of other opportunities in the past if they wanted to do away with me."

Erica still didn't look convinced. "So you haven't ticked any of them off recently?"

Trevor smiled and shook his head. "Again, the only one here who fits that bill is you."

Erica played in his hair for another moment even though Trevor could sense that she'd said her piece. Maybe he was getting to her after all. Then she slipped from his embrace and stepped away. Or not.

Trevor tried to hold her hand again, but Erica avoided his grasp. She put an arm around his waist instead. "I need my hands free. Just in case." Who was he to argue if she'd prefer to be joined at the hip?

Trevor kept track of every person he and Erica greeted while they made their way toward the kitchen. He'd also noted that his father was missing. Along with his best cronies. Trevor figured they were holed up in the basement watching a game or something. His father would emerge once most of the town had left. There was no doubt Trevor had gotten his social butterfly gene from his mother. Once she'd finished the food preparation, he knew she'd be outside in the thick of things.

He opened the door to the small enclosed back porch for Erica and felt her tension ease a bit once she saw no one was there. He was beginning to understand her concerns. She couldn't just relax and enjoy things like he could. She had to stay vigilant. And after that seven hour drive, he could just imagine what it was costing her. He had to figure out how to give her a respite.

* * * *

Erica wondered why she was nervous all of a sudden. It wasn't like she was meeting his mother as a real girlfriend. She tried to tell herself it was because if she failed in her job, she'd have to give the woman some devastating news. Even though the excuse rang false in her own ears, Erica was determined to stick with it. The alternative was just too much for her to consider.

Trevor held the door for Erica to step inside the actual house. The first thing that hit her was the warm scent of cinnamon and apples. Trevor gave her an approving look when she sniffed in appreciation.

"Mom's baking. Apple pie is her specialty."

"It smells amazing."

"Wait until you taste it."

Trevor ushered her into the big, sunny kitchen. A woman squealed and dropped the pie she'd been taking from the oven onto the floor and ran to his waiting arms. Identifying the grinning woman with the long blonde hair as his mother in an instant, Erica turned her attention to the other occupants of the room. She figured the three older women were close friends of his mother's if their apron-wrapped waists and flour dusted noses were any indication. The youngest, Erica recognized as Marcy. She didn't look happy to see her, and her smile turned pretty brittle when Erica entered the kitchen.

Trevor pulled Erica into the greeting. Surprise flitted over his mother's face and she glanced at Marcy before it settled into a welcoming smile. "Erica, this is my mom, Abigail Cole. Mom, this is my friend, Erica." Erica extended her hand to the woman, but she was surprised to be pulled into a big hug instead.

"Erica, it's so nice to meet you. You'll have to tell me all about you and Trevor. But first, let's get these pies out to the masses. The sooner they eat them, the sooner they'll go home and I can visit with my boy."

Abigail went to retrieve the dropped pie. A red haired woman who looked sort of familiar shooed her away. "I'll get that."

"Thanks, hon." Abigail scooped up a tray of pies and

headed for the door. Without delay, Marcy opened it for her. "Erica, doll, you know Cam's wife?" At Erica's nodded greeting, Abigail continued. "And this is Hope, Cam's mom." That explained the familiarity. Hope nodded at Erica while she dumped pie remains in the garbage and sent a questioning look toward Marcy. She grabbed her own tray of pies.

"Call me, Abby." She shifted the pie tray on her arm and added some napkins to her burden. Trevor sprung to help her, but she waved him away.

"We're gonna check on Dad then we'll be down."

"You know where they are. Tell me if they need anything." At the mere mention of his father, Abigail seemed to just light up. Erica marveled at the realization that after forty plus years, they must still be on their honeymoon. She would love to fall in love like that. Before she could stop herself, Erica found herself wondering if she could fall for Trevor that way.

"Marcy, could you grab the ice cream on the way out? Thanks, hon," Abigail called on her way out the door.

"Save me some pie," Trevor called after his mother.

"You know I did," she sing-songed back.

Trevor grinned.

Marcy grabbed the ice cream and scrambled after the other women. Trevor and Erica shared a shrug.

* * * *

Trevor led Erica through the first floor of the house. She marveled at the myriad of photos covering almost every available surface. She halted in her tracks and backed up. Trevor opened a door, and then looked at her with a puzzled frown.

"What's up?"

A grin split Erica's face from ear to ear while she studied an old photo of Trevor. He couldn't have been more than three or four, but he was on a stage gripping a microphone for all he was worth. He'd gone down to his knees, thrown his head and arm back while obviously holding a note. A rock star in training. She turned to the grown up version.

"This is priceless."

He came back to see what she was looking at and grimaced. "No matter how often I hide that photo, my mom always finds another one. I think she has a stash somewhere."

"Why would you want to hide it? It's perfect. The quintessential Trevor Cole." Erica leaned closer to read, "Tiny Tots Talent Extravaganza and Competition. Did you win?"

He shook his head and pointed to a very sour looking little girl in the corner of the photo. "Betsy Manderhoffen. She sung Amazing Grace, badly, just like she did every year. And won, just like she did every year." Trevor considered the photo again. "Her mom ran the competition, too. That may have had something to do with it."

Erica laughed and gave him a little squeeze. "And what did you sing?"

"'She's a brick. house!'" Trevor sang and Erica doubled over in laughter. "Hey! I'll have you know, I rocked the house."

"You don't think it was at all inappropriate for what, a three or four year old, to sing?"

Trevor contemplated the picture again. His own laughter surfaced. "To be fair, I believed the lyrics were actually about a brick house." He gave a tiny shrug when a grin split his face. "No wonder all the judges looked like they were sucking on lemons."

Erica cracked up again. Trevor grabbed her hand and ushered her along. "Just you remember this when I see embarrassing photos of you."

"They don't exist." Erica laughed even harder while he led her downstairs to a finished basement.

They were greeted by a hearty chorus of hellos from the three older men occupying the room. Trying not to be obtrusive, Erica placed herself between Trevor and the others until she could feel them out.

"Hey, everybody. This is Erica." Trevor ushered her toward the biggest man in the bunch. He still had mostly jet black hair with the tiniest streaks of grey and kind green eyes. Erica didn't need Trevor's intro to realize that this was his father. The older man shook Erica's hand with a firm, but gentle grip with his large hand.

"This is my dad, Cliff Cole. Dad, my friend, Erica."

"Pleasure to meet you," Erica said. And it was. Other than the jet black hair, it was just like meeting Trevor all over again.

"I'd like to say Trevor's told me all about you, but I'm afraid I can't." He shot a pointed look at Trevor before settling his piercing stare on Erica. She got the distinct sense he was sizing her up. Trying to ascertain how she felt about his son. Erica couldn't say she blamed him. Trevor must have women falling all over him. It was a father's right to be a little protective. Though Erica had to admit she'd expected it more from his mother.

"I'm afraid there's not much to tell. I swim in Trevor's show. Since the next venue was cancelled, I found myself at loose ends. Trevor convinced me to tag along. So here I am." Erica couldn't put a finger on why she couldn't bring herself to lie to his father. She imagined it was because he reminded her too much of her own. She'd never been able to lie to him, either.

Trevor draped an arm around Erica's shoulders and pulled her away from Cliff. "I already have my work cut out for me trying to sweep her off her feet. You mind postponing the third degree until after my devious plan to show her all about what a great guy I am works?"

Cliff stared at his son for a long moment. It seemed to Erica that some unspoken understanding passed between them that she couldn't quite put her finger on. Cliff smiled at Erica and teased, "My son is a great guy. The greatest."

"So you say," Erica retorted, glad the awkward moment had passed.

Cliff introduced her to his friends. James and Richard seemed to be pretty solid guys. Erica settled in to watch the dynamics of the group. It wasn't long before they sucked her into their camaraderie. If she were really Trevor's girlfriend, she'd have been pleased that she'd won his father over so thoroughly.

The hours melted away and Erica was surprised to see that evening was becoming nightfall when Trevor led her outside. Erica was even more stunned to realize that despite Abby's claim that the guests would be leaving once the pie ran out, it seemed that more folk had shown up. And there wasn't a lick of pie to be seen.

Erica studied the joyful people laughing and dancing and carrying on and had another surprising epiphany. A smile quivered on her lips when she squeezed Trevor's hand and leaned close to his ear.

"I hate to strike a blow to your delicate male ego, but I don't think all these people are here to see you."

He snaked an arm around her waist to hold her close. It was

a lot more comfortable than she wanted to admit so she concentrated on his words instead.

"You're right. Any occasion for a party is a good one. I just happened to be the catalyst this time."

Erica nodded and stepped away. Something in his eyes flashed and Erica was sure she didn't want to know what it was so she turned to look at the crowd again. It brought a smile to her face to see his mother behaving like the social butterfly of social butterflies. Trevor followed her gaze.

"I hope she didn't fool you with all that "sooner they go home" nonsense." Trevor's breath whispered across her cheek making her long to lean into him. Not sure what was in her expression, Erica kept her face toward Abigail.

"Of course not," she lied.

Trevor laughed. "Let's grab a bite."

The surprises just kept rolling in when Trevor led her to four huge tables crisscrossed in the middle of the tent. Each table was loaded down with food, all of it homemade by the looks of it. Having only snacked all day, Erica's mouth began to water.

"I thought it was just pie." She looked at Trevor.

"The pie was just to tide folks over until the main event." He gestured toward the tables. "Where do you wanna start?"

Plates loaded down with yummy goodness, Erica and Trevor headed to find seats. They snagged a couple near a makeshift stage where a rowdy country band was playing their hearts out. They settled into some empty seats at a table, and then Erica sampled a bit of everything from Trevor's plate before starting on her own.

"You know you have you a plate, too." Erica just smiled and dug into her own food. His expression lit in understanding. "It's okay if you take some down time."

Erica met his eye. "No. It isn't."

Trevor heaved an inward sigh. Then he decided to make a game of it. He speared some of her potato salad.

"Hey!" Erica protested.

Trevor shrugged. "What's good for the goose . . ."

Erica shifted her plate away, but he followed. Erica struck back and polished off his baked beans. They turned into little kids while they sparred over each other's food. Erica had ketchup on her nose and Trevor had mustard on his chin when a burly man clapped him on the shoulder. "Alrighty now, boy. Your belly oughta be full enough to get up on that stage and show us how it's done."

Trevor grinned. "Y'all not ready for me, Uncle Charlie." He begged off even while he stood. Erica caught his arm. A challenging look flashed in his eyes. It turned to surprise when she wiped the mustard away with a napkin. His eyes heated while he studied her another long moment. Erica knew she should, but she refused to look away. The older man nudged Trevor, breaking the spell. With a grin, he headed to the stage with Charlie.

Since they'd been sitting near the stage to begin with, Erica didn't feel the need to move closer. Trevor smiled at her when he picked up a guitar and perched on a stool, and she had the feeling he'd known he'd be performing soon and wanted her to have a good seat.

Expecting to hear one of his rock tunes, Erica was surprised when he launched into a silly country tune. Trevor outdid himself adding a twang to his voice while he belted out the crazy lyrics. Erica had never heard the song before and suspected he was making it up on the spot. The crowd caught on to the chorus and sang it along with him. Several people headed for a makeshift dance floor to shimmy and shake with the music.

Trevor moved from one tune to the next. She didn't think it was possible, but it seemed that each song was funnier than the previous. Trevor had everyone within earshot eating out of the palm of his hand and looked to be enjoying every minute. If Erica had thought she'd seen him in his element when they were performing in his big over produced shows, she'd been sadly mistaken.

When Trevor wound it up, thunderous applause greeted him.

He held up his hands, accepting the applause at first and then tried to quiet it. "All you fellows cuddle up with your best girl. I've got something for you." Trevor strummed the opening notes of a ballad.

One by one, couples moved to the dance floor to sway in gentle rhythm while Trevor's mellow voice washed over them. Erica liked the way Trevor had of engaging all the members of his audience. He made them feel like he was playing just for them. At least that's how she felt. She found herself humming along with him. Something about the sweet song tugged at the cords of her memory. Erica's breath hitched. It was the song he'd played the first time he'd seen her swim. She couldn't imagine when he'd had time to finish it. But it was beautiful. Oh how she wished she had a pool right now.

She looked at Trevor and found him looking back at her. She could see the secret question in his smile. She nodded her answer. He winked at her. When he launched into the next verse, Erica knew it would be easy to love a guy like him. So it was no wonder that she did.

Chapter Twelve

Erica sat ramrod straight. All of a sudden, the air seemed to have disappeared when the idea crossed her consciousness. It had been her imagination. There was no possibility she could be in love with Trevor Cole. First, it was totally unprofessional. She was nothing if not professional. Second, he was her boss. Her fake boss, but still her boss nonetheless. Third, he . . . Erica found she couldn't come up with a viable third. She could say that he was always surrounded by too many women. But having lived with him like she had, she knew that he was very controlled on that front. Still, she wanted to say that all those other women would always be competing with her for his attention. But he had a way of having eyes only for her. Just like he was doing now.

She replayed their entire acquaintance in her mind. Erica knew he was attracted to her. The memory of their botched kiss still curled her toes. But she figured she'd gotten through to him about not splitting her focus. Now, Erica had to wonder.

She remembered all the little "suggestions" he'd made. She considered all the times he'd invented a reason to touch her. She reflected on how he'd come to her defense when Dani attacked her then later insisted that Dani had no right to be mad even after she'd told him the whole story. Guys didn't go to all that trouble unless they were trying to get you into bed or they loved you. And she was willing to bet Trevor didn't love her. He couldn't.

* * * *

Trepidation settled in Trevor's gut while he watched the emotions play out over Erica's face. He could've sworn she was touched that he'd finished this song for her. But now, by the looks of things, she couldn't be thinking anything good. Wanting to get her out of the crowd had him wrapping up the song before he'd gotten to the third verse. Charlie tried to get him to give them another, but Trevor played the tired card. Like he'd known she would, Erica met him along the side of the stage.

"What's wrong?" she asked once she got to his side.

"Nothing. Just ready to call it a day is all."

She nodded in agreement, but tensed when he put his arm around her. "We passed a hotel on the way in. We'll . . ."

"Whoa." Trevor stopped to look at her. "We're staying here. You knew that when we left."

"That was before the entire county showed up here. Look around you, Trevor." Erica made a nonchalant gesture around the ranch, but Trevor could read how wound up she was easier than a page of sheet music. "I cannot guarantee your security here."

"Guarantee my . . . this is my parents' house. I grew up here. If I'm not secure here, I won't be secure anywhere."

* * * *

Barely holding on to her civility, Erica pulled out of his grasp and looked at him. "What if someone here slipped into the house and left a nice surprise for you?"

"These are my closest relatives and friends. I can't believe you'd think that of them."

"I can't believe you wouldn't." Erica knew she was being unreasonable, but she needed to get out of there. Everywhere she looked, she could imagine Trevor growing up. All of his firsts. All of the things that had made him the man he was. It only made her long for him all the more. Hoping to spare herself that anguish and regain some equilibrium, Erica wanted a minute away. She needed a minute away.

She was sure that once she got to neutral territory her brain would start working again. Better yet, she could go over the report Jason had sent her yesterday again. Maybe she'd missed something. Maybe she could find some lead they'd both missed. She would point it out to Jason, he'd follow up, the case would be solved and she and Trevor could go their separate ways. Yes. That would be the best outcome for them all. So why did her heart clench at the thought of never seeing Trevor again?

Deciding it was just a little bit of heartburn, Erica pressed on. "Just be reasonable, Trevor."

* * * *

He folded his arms across his chest and dug in his heels. "Unless you plan on knocking me out and slinging me over your shoulder to carry me away, I'm not going anywhere."

Trevor prayed she couldn't do just that. He wasn't sure what had gotten into Erica. She'd known his plan to stay at the ranch from the beginning. He wasn't in the mood to cajole her around to his way of thinking.

"You know, that can be arranged," she informed him with a glint in her eye that he knew meant business.

"What can be arranged?" Both Trevor and Erica snapped to attention when his mother joined them. Sensing an ally, Trevor slung an arm around her shoulders.

"Nothing, Ma. We were just talking over where to stay tonight."

"Nonsense. There's plenty of room for the both of you here. Don't give it another thought." Abigail smiled at Erica, but it was obvious she figured more was going here.

* * * *

Erica found her smile. "I just don't want to put anybody out."

"This is Trevor's home. He's always welcome home. But if you feel that way, you're welcome to find another place to sleep."

The unspoken 'by yourself' came through loud and clear. Erica was the scum of the earth because it was obvious Abby believed she was trying to take her son from her. There was no way she could explain the real situation. She glanced at Trevor's gloating face. And reconsidered. "Well, I'm afraid it's not that simple. I'm actually his. . ."

"Maybe we should go to a hotel," Trevor interrupted with a glare at Erica. The look that passed between them was designed to let him know that she meant business. She was prepared to blow her cover if need be. He'd already told her how his mom would freak out to learn he needed a bodyguard.

His mother gave him such a heartbroken look that it tore at Erica's insides. Still, she couldn't back down. Not this time. She knew he would spare his mom the truth at all costs.

"A hotel? I've barely gotten to see you. I had breakfast all planned and everything."

"We'll be here a couple of days," Trevor reassured her.

"That's not the same. I can't take care of you if you're not here to be taken care of." Abigail patted his cheek. Okay, so Erica was the most horrid person on the face of the earth taking Trevor away from his family like this. But wouldn't it be worse if the guy got to him and took him away forever? She had to stand her ground.

She was determined not to be swayed by Trevor's sad eyes. So she said, "You're right. He came home to visit, so he'll visit. We'll be happy to stay here."

Abigail gave Erica a look of gratitude mixed with don't-play-me-little-girl and she knew she'd been bested. She also had the feeling that her estimation had just dropped lower than a slug's belly in his mother's eyes. Erica couldn't do anything about that. Even though it hurt, she had to remember she wasn't here to make friends. She was here to keep the woman's son safe. Still, it saddened Erica that she'd made an enemy of someone she'd have loved to call friend.

Trevor bid his mother good night, and Erica followed him to get their bags from the car then inside the house and up to his old room. After a careful sweep of the inside, she allowed him to enter. She didn't really think that the place was unsafe, but she wasn't about to let Trevor in on it. He'd scored enough off her for one day.

Speaking of scoring, she took note of the bed. The full sized mattress would've been huge while he was growing up. Now that he was grown she was sure he'd take more than his share. She could fit, but only if she was snug against him. Given where her thoughts were heading, that was the worst idea on the planet.

"This'll be fine. You'll see." Trevor broke the strained silence that was stretching between them.

Erica just stood and studied him. For such a long time that he fidgeted. At last, she dropped her gaze and pulled her bag to a spot in front of the door to stretch out on the floor.

Trevor frowned. "You can't sleep down there. It'll be cozy, but we can share the bed."

Erica never bothered to look at him. "I have to secure the door. There's no lock."

* * * *

She never ceased to amaze him with her dedication, but enough was enough.

"No need to sulk because you didn't get your way." Trevor sat on the bed and pulled off his boots.

Erica sat up one inch at a time and looked at him. "Sulk? Is that what you think I'm doing?" She was, but there was no reason for him to know that. "I think in all this hand holding and food playing and whatever you forgot why I'm here."

"I haven't forgotten. Not for a second. And I can't believe you were about to tell my mother. What's wrong with you?"

"What's wrong with me?" Furious, Erica popped to her feet. "I'm not the one with the death wish. I mean that's the only thing it could be that has you thwarting me at every turn."

Trevor stood to square off with her. "Thwarting? Sweetheart, take a look around. I've made every concession possible so you could do your job."

In no way intimidated, Erica stepped to him and put her hands on her hips. "Except follow the most basic instructions that would allow me to guard you effectively."

Trevor stepped nose to nose with her and spread his arms. "You wanna guard me? I'm right here. Guard away."

Toe to toe, nose to nose and everything in between, Trevor and Erica stared each other down. The anger simmering between them ignited into something else. Erica wasn't sure who closed that last millimeter of distance, but suddenly their mouths were fused in a passionate kiss.

Erica excused herself for kissing him back with everything

she had in her because it happened so fast. When Trevor grasped her upper arms and drove her backward until he pressed her against the door she didn't resist. Instead, Erica brought her hands up to tangle in his hair when she pulled him closer. With one leg, she hooked his hips, trapping him against her.

* * * *

Trevor would've smiled against her lips if he wasn't engaged in the serious business of kissing her thoroughly. He wasn't going anywhere. Not when this was where he wanted to be more than anywhere else in the world. The fact that she worked for him was dwarfed compared to the heat building between them. They could work it out. Now that he was positive she had feelings for him, hope sparked in his heart — along with other things.

* * * *

Feeling exactly how ready he was for her against her most intimate parts gave Erica pause. She couldn't do this. Not and do her job to the best of her ability. She turned her head to break the kiss, but he was undeterred. He simply kissed his way down her neck. When his hand made its way to her breast for a caress, Erica sighed. She had to get out now. Before it was too late.

"Trevor, no." With flat palms she tried to push him away. She didn't have enough leverage and he was determined to stay put. He did pause long enough to look at her with passion filled eyes.

"You can't be serious." To prove his point, he brought both hands up to stroke her already straining nipples. He smiled. "See?"

Erica batted his hands away and rolled to the side. Trevor stumbled against the door in the sudden absence of her body. He just managed to catch his balance.

* * * *

"This thing between us . . . it's not going to go away." Trevor turned to face her, unconcerned that his pants had quite a tent in the front. "Don't you think we've fought it long enough?"

"No. I don't."

"I admit we have some things to work out."

"Don't you think they should be worked out before we add

another complication?" Erica risked getting close to him again to open the door. "I'll be in the hall if you need anything."

"You know what I need, Erica." Trevor relented and pushed the door closed. "Fine. But you don't have to sleep in the hall. I'll behave."

"Maybe it's not you I'm worried about." Her statement shocked Trevor enough that his pressure on the door slackened enough that she could escape. Erica fled into the hallway and pulled the door closed behind her.

* * * *

She sat on the floor and rested her head on her knees. She didn't look up when she heard the door ease open behind her.

"Please, Trevor. Just give me some space. Please."

Tension still thickened the air between them. He knelt beside her to whisper, "This is far from over, Erica."

Trevor kissed her shoulder. "Good night." He pushed the door closed, but she noticed that he didn't latch it. She pulled it the rest of the way herself. The last thing she needed was that invitation.

Trying to distract herself, Erica checked her text messages. She was dying to hear that Jason had caught the guy. The sooner that happened, the sooner Erica could get back to her regularly scheduled life and Trevor could stop pretending she was more than nearby and available.

Jason's message buoyed her spirits though it wasn't exactly what she'd hoped for. They had an eye on a suspect. Jason promised to keep her up-to-date. Erica studied the photo attached to the message. The man, one Edward Worthingham, looked so ordinary and plain, but there was an arrogant look in his eye. She shook her head. No matter. He'd be in custody soon enough. They'd already tied him to having paid for the bomb and the snakes. She was almost free. With that suddenly depressing thought, Erica nestled against the doorjamb and tried to relax.

* * * *

Inside the room, Trevor was having trouble getting his mind to calm down. Prowling the area that had once been his childhood haven did nothing to relax him. He could use a cold shower. But that meant stepping over Erica in the doorway where he knew she'd be because her sense of duty wouldn't allow her to go any farther. Besides, he'd promised her space. And he intended to give it to her.

Trevor paused in his pacing and considered the window. It would have to do. He strode to it and slid it open without a sound. It brought a smile to his face when he rested on the sill and inhaled fresh, but chilly air. That and his memories of sneaking in and out of his room via this route when he was young had the desired effect. After a few more moments, he left the open window to climb into bed. While he got comfortable, regrets that Erica was sleeping on the uncomfortable hallway floor assaulted him. Vowing to make it up to her, he drifted off to sleep.

* * * *

"Erica?" Erica opened her eyes to see Abigail standing over her. It was a really bad sign that she hadn't even heard the woman approach. How exhausted must she be? "What are you doing out here?"

Erica sat up and tried to ignore her protesting muscles. She wasn't sure if it was a sign of age or a testimony to the comfort of the hardwood floor. "Just resting. Did you need something? Did you want Trevor?"

Abigail planted her hands on her hips. "You don't raise five children and not learn to recognize when your questions are dodged."

"I'm not . . . I'm just," Erica faked a yawn hoping it gave her confusion credibility while she tried to come up with a suitable excuse.

"Dodging." Abigail's expression softened, and she knelt next to Erica. "That son of mine knows better than to treat you like this. If you fought, why didn't he put you in one of the other bedrooms?"

"I'm fine where I am, Mrs. Cole." Erica held the woman's gaze the best she could. Finally, Abigail stood.

"I was headed downstairs to start breakfast. Why don't you join me? And what happened to Abby?"

"I really can't, Abby." Erica shifted trying to relieve the numbness in her backside.

Abigail studied her for another moment, and then nodded. She turned to continue toward the stairs.

"Mrs. . . . . Abby?" Erica waited until the older woman looked at her. "I'm sorry about last night. I wanted you to know that I'd never try to separate you and your son."

Abigail gave her a tight smile then disappeared down the stairs. Erica dropped her head against the door with a quiet thump. That went well. She tried to settle in for a few more Z's, but her instincts went on high alert. Ignoring her creaking muscles, she stood and listened through the door. A frown furrowed her brow when she could make out whispers. Trevor didn't talk in his sleep. Erica pushed the door open. Her heart thumped wildly in her chest when she saw a dark figure standing over Trevor's prone body on the bed.

Without a second thought, Erica launched herself across the room and took the man down with a flying kick.

* * * *

Trevor sat up and sleepily rubbed his eyes. He didn't quite trust his vision when he saw Erica locked in battle with an assailant. Not wanting to believe she'd been right about finding a hotel, he kicked his way free of the tangled covers and stood.

The figure didn't stay down long. He sprung from his back to his feet and launched a flurry of punches and kicks at Erica. She never shied away. A couple connected, making Trevor cringe, but she held her ground. When Erica continued to back away, the figure continued a blitz of punches.

Once she got near the wall, Erica timed her defense so a punch that would have done her major damage connected with the solid logs framing the window sill. While the guy took a necessary moment to regroup, Erica let loose with her own attack.

Using her feet for the most part, she drove the figure into the closet door. Trevor could only watch in awe. She was amazing to behold. He'd hate to be the guy who'd burst in on them. Except, the attacker turned the tables on her. She fired off a kick, but he caught her leg and flipped her over.

Trevor flinched when she landed on her back with a soft "oooofff." The man tried to get out of the corner by diving over her and tumbling to his feet. But Erica caught a handful of his sleeve.

The sudden shift in his body weight sent the guy sprawling across the bed. His sleeve ripped clean off revealing a heavily muscled arm filled with tattoos. He bounced and landed on the floor with a thump.

Trevor gasped when he recognized the tattoos in the moonlight. He rushed into the fray. He pulled Erica away from the attacker when she tried to bring her mighty heel down on the guy's groin.

"What are you doing? Let go!" She demanded while Trevor fought to hold her still.

"Cut it out! Both of you!" Trevor commanded when the guy got to his feet. Trevor knew he'd be furious. And that brought a smile to his face.

The guy flipped on the overhead light to reveal a scowl on his chiseled face. "What the hell, Trev? I come in to say hello and this is how you treat me?"

"It's your own fault, Jordy. And you just got your little Navy Officer butt kicked. By a girl." Trevor grinned from ear to ear while Jordan continued to scowl at them both. Erica looked over her shoulder at Trevor.

"Jordy? As in your brother?"

"She didn't kick my butt. I wasn't going full out."

Trevor laughed and released Erica. "Yeah right. Erica, this is Jordan. Jordan, Erica."

Trevor and Jordan shared a manly hug, and then Trevor socked Jordan in the gut. "For the record, I don't appreciate you wailing on my girl like that."

"She attacked me. What's your issue, lady?"

Erica planted her hands on her hips to glare at Jordan. "My issue? You came in a window! How is that normal?"

Seeing the utter fury in Erica's eyes that was mirrored in Jordan's, Trevor stepped between the two of them. "Children, children . . ."

Erica spun on Trevor and interrupted. "Children? Do not patronize me, Trevor."

"I'm not patronizing, I'm just . . . things have gotten a little out of control."

"A little? Oh that's rich. And who do you think is responsible for that?" She planted her hands on her hips while she issued the challenge.

Trevor frowned. "Surely you don't think I'm . . ."

"That's exactly what I think. From the very beginning, you've insisted on having things your way. And look where it's gotten us."

"Okay, so there've been a few bumps along the way."

"A few bumps? What if he hadn't been your brother?" She poked him in the chest. Hard. "I'm done coddling. I'm the bodyguard; you're the client. You will obey my every command without even looking like you're going to question it. You're not going to offer alternatives, suggestions, or even fashion tips."

"Wait. She's your bodyguard? Mom said . . ." Jordan looked between the two of them with a smirk.

"Not talking to you." Erica whirled around and nailed Jordan with such a harsh look that the bigger man retreated a pace. She turned back to Trevor. "That's the first thing to go. These stupid cover stories. I'm not your swimmer. I'm not your girlfriend. I'm here for one reason and one reason only. That's to protect your sorry behind even from you if necessary."

"Then what am I supposed to tell everybody?"

"Completely up to you and no longer my problem. Though, might I suggest the truth?"

"Mom'll have a fit . . ."

"She'll get over it. You will remain attached to my hip at all times. Where I go, you go."

"Does that include the shower? Wanna protect me, too?" Without even bothering to look back, Erica shoved her elbow in Jordan's gut.

"Do you understand these rules as I have laid them out for you?" Erica stood and waited for Trevor's response. He stared at her through narrowed eyes obviously not liking anything she'd just announced.

"And if I don't?"

Erica shrugged. "You didn't hire me, and you can't fire me. I won't let you stop me from doing my job. I will handcuff you to me if need be."

"Dude! She has handcuffs." Jordan rubbed his meaty hands together in delight.

"Fine," Trevor spat.

"Fine," Erica echoed.

"I'm telling ya, dude. Go for the handcuffs," Jordan encouraged.

With an eye roll, Erica spun on her heel and headed for the door just as it was shoved open. Cliff loomed large in the doorway with an unhappy scowl on his face.

"What's all this racket in here?" His face lightened a little when his gaze landed on Jordan, but he held onto his scowl. Trevor and his brother adopted innocent expressions telling Erica that they'd gone through this many times in the past.

Jordan spoke up first. "Trevor's girlfriend got a little rowdy." Erica turned a disbelieving look on him. He shrugged. "Sorry, Dad."

"That's not . . ." Erica tried to defend herself, but Trevor talked over her.

". . . entirely true. Jordan startled us is all." Trevor slung an arm around Erica and gave her a squeeze. She shot him a warning look. "We didn't mean to wake you and Mom."

"Good to see you, Jordan. Now, get to your room." He stepped to the side and swept a hand the direction Jordan was to go. The man obeyed without hesitation. Still, he threw a smirk over his shoulder at Erica when he passed. Cliff turned his attention back to Erica and Trevor. "You two, back to sleep. I don't wanna hear another peep outta any of ya."

"Yessir."

A few hours later, they all sat down to breakfast where Abigail's amazing cooking threatened to cheer Erica right up. But another "what if" would cross her mind and she went right back to the fear infused place she'd inhabited since she'd found Jordan standing over Trevor. What if it hadn't been Jordan? What if she hadn't run away? The list went around and around. Each time it ended with her failure that could've cost Trevor his life.

Needing time to sort through everything, Erica was happy to let Jordan relieve her for the day after she'd learned of his impressive naval background. At nightfall, Trevor found her lounging under a tree checking Jason's progress on her Treo.

"You get reception out here?"

Not daring to go into detail about Trecam's vast resources that allowed her to get reception almost anywhere in the world,

Erica just smiled and discreetly put the device away. "I see you survived the day with your brother."

Trevor joined her on the ground and handed her a plate of food. She nodded her thanks, but put the plate aside.

"What's wrong? I tested it all out myself."

Erica found herself cracking a tiny smile before she could help it.

"Oh good. There's hope for you yet." Trevor picked up the plate and held a forkful of green beans to her lips. "I know for a fact that you haven't eaten since breakfast. So here."

"You don't know for a fact." Erica pushed his hand away.

Trevor sighed and abandoned the plate. "Don't do this to yourself, Erica."

"I left you unprotected. There's no excuse for . . ." Erica shook her head and stood to pace so there was some physical distance between them.

Trevor refused to let her go that easy. He blocked her path and held her still so she had to look at him. "What matters is you were there if I needed you." Trevor rubbed Erica's arms. "Just like you always are."

What a complicated statement. Becoming more complicated by the second, she admitted and enjoyed each pass his hands made over her skin. He must have read her mind in her eyes because his stare heated while he studied her. She shook her head and backed out of his grasp. "Trevor, no. What you're feeling—it's just gratitude. Like you just said, I've been there for you in difficult times. It's not surprising that you fancy yourself attracted to me."

Trevor shook his head. He closed the distance between them again. "I know gratitude. And sweetheart, this ain't it." He lowered his head bit by bit for a kiss even while he released her arms. She knew she should move. She wanted to move. Nothing was stopping her from moving. She didn't have her back against a wall. He wasn't holding her. She could definitely move. And she did.

Right toward him.

Chapter Thirteen

Erica's lips met Trevor's in a kiss so exquisite that it stole the breath from her on contact. She could feel him tremble with restraint with the simple touch of his lips to hers, and then his tongue. He kept his hands locked behind his back giving her an out. That very fact just made her not want it all the more.

Silencing her voice of common sense, Erica slid her arms around his neck and stepped closer. When she molded her curves to his solid frame, she could feel that he was ready for more than a simple kiss. Yet, he continued to allow her to take the lead. He whimpered in protest when she broke the kiss and laid her head on his shoulder. At last, he allowed his arms to loosely circle her.

"There're so many reasons why we can't do this."

"I believe we decided to work through the complications, not give up on them," Trevor reminded her in a gentle tone.

"And you think right now is a good time to work out complications?" Erica broke away and leveled an amused smile at him.

Trevor gave her a sheepish shrug. "Can you blame me if I just want to get on with my life? With you in it."

Erica held up a hand and shook her head. "Let's just back off a minute." She paused to choose her words with care. "We might be close to an arrest."

* * * *

"You found him? When? Where? How did you have time?" The questions just tumbled out of his mouth. All of a sudden, he remembered. She was teamed up with a staff of world class investigators. Her part of the assignment had been to keep him safe on the front lines while the rest of the team ran down the leads she passed to them. He was impressed with their efficiency. He didn't want to know if they'd pulled resources from other cases to finish his so quickly. He was just glad they had. Then he and Erica would be free to explore the passion between them.

"Let's just give it a moment." She shrugged. "When you don't need me, we'll see if you . . . need me."

Trevor smiled. There was no doubt in his mind that he'd always need her. And love her. And boy was he looking forward to loving her. He had to admit that he was impressed she had never broken her cover. Wouldn't she be surprised when she learned that he'd known who she was all this time? He couldn't wait to tell her.

* * * *

Later that night, Trevor watched Erica root around in her canvas bag once the house quieted and everyone'd retired to their rooms. After that morning's excitement, Trevor half expected her to insist they go to a hotel again. She'd had all day to announce she was his bodyguard, but she hadn't.

He took that to be a good sign. Along with the kiss they'd shared later, things were definitely going his way.

Trying not to gloat, he tried to figure out what she was doing with the tape at the window. In a lot of ways, she reminded him of Jordan. They had the same resourcefulness and resilience. But she sure was better looking.

A twinge of jealousy stabbed Trevor's heart. What if she and Jordan ended up hitting it off? After all, they were in sort of the same line of work. Whereas Trevor was just the wimpy singer who couldn't even take care of himself. He didn't have the slightest clue what she was up to at the window he realized when she stretched a tiny cord across the sill. Not only would Jordan know, but he'd be able to offer suggestions to make it better.

Trevor grunted and slunk down in the bed making the frame creak. She turned from her task to look at him.

"You say something?"

"No . . . I . . ." Trevor searched for something to say. "I . . . uh . . . thank you. It's really cool of you to let us stay here. I know you'd prefer a hotel."

"A hotel is easier to secure." She stood back to examine her handy work. "But your mom . . . I don't want her to feel left out. And now that I know everyone in the house, I can rest a little easier." She kicked off her shoes and climbed in on the opposite half of the bed. "Besides, Jordan'll have my back if need be. Despite what a Neanderthal he is, I can tell he loves you."

Trevor fought the scowl that leapt to his face. Jordan. She was totally into him. Trevor tucked his feet in the bed and lay on his side to face her. But Jordan didn't have one thing he did. Propinquity. And he was going to use it.

"You notice how we always seem to end up in the same bed." He chuckled. "Or cave floor."

She yawned. "It does happen a little too often, doesn't it? I'm just glad you're a gentleman." She tossed him a look over her shoulder. "Most of the time."

Trevor mumbled, "Most of the time." He snuggled closer and threw an arm over her.

"Trevor? What are you doing?"

Trevor didn't answer. He feigned sleep even while his hand covered her braless breast. He loved how it fit just perfectly in his large palm with just a bit of overflow.

"Fine," he heard her mutter and figured that she was going to stay put. His eyes flew open when cold metal snapped around the wrist attached to the offending hand. In the same instant, his arm was pulled up over his head, and he heard another snap. He looked up and saw that she'd handcuffed his arm to the white headboard bars. Scandalized, he looked at her. She gazed back impassively.

"It's been three days since I've had a decent night's rest. Since you seem determined to make it four, I see I'm going to have to nip this in the bud."

Trevor twisted trying to get untangled from the awkward

position in which he now found himself. Seeing he was just making things worse, he stopped. "Okay, okay. I give. I'll behave. I promise."

Erica slid out of bed and smiled down at him. She pulled the covers all the way to the foot of the bed exposing him from head to toe. "I know you will." She turned to dig in her bag again. Trevor enjoyed the view of her perfect behind when she bent over. "I think I'm going to grab another bite of pie before I turn in. In the meantime, try to relax. When I get back, we'll both sleep."

"Wait a minute! What makes you think I won't scream bloody murder the moment you're gone?"

"You can if you want. I'll just explain to your mother when she runs in to check on her precious baby boy — 'cause I know my little booby trap won't do all that much to deter a determined mother — how we were playing a kinky sex game and you couldn't wait for me to get back with the whipped cream." Erica gave him a sweet smile. "Sound good?"

"She'd never believe that."

Erica's eyes swept over his sprawled form. Her eyes lingered on the bulge just below the waistband of his pajamas. "Really?" She met his eyes and smiled.

Trevor was floored to learn of this little devious streak of Erica's. And more than a little turned on. Determined not to give her the satisfaction of hiding what she did to him, Trevor twisted his hips so they were flat on the bed with the bulge proudly at attention. He studied her reaction and was thrilled to see that she wasn't as unaffected as she was trying to pretend.

"So what happens when someone walks in? We're a pretty open family, you know."

She drug her gaze back to meet his and tossed a nine volt battery in the air and caught it. "I'm planning to lock the door." With that statement, she fled the room. Lock the door? It didn't have a lock. And what booby trap? He heard some rustling on the other side of the door for a bit then all was quiet.

Trevor peered around his arm that was locked across his body to his saluting manhood and sighed. "So how 'bout those Yankees?"

* * * *

Erica slipped into the darkened kitchen and noticed a bulky silhouette by the window. Not eager of a repeat performance of their earlier tussle, she announced, "It's just me."

"I know," was Jordan's quiet reply. He turned around to face her. She heard the amusement in his voice when he said, "So what happened to your shadow?"

Erica was glad the darkness would cover her grimace. "He's otherwise . . . engaged."

Jordan's soft chuckle had her relaxing a little. Not completely, though. While she knew he would protect Trevor with everything in him, she wasn't sure if he saw her as a threat or not. That's why his next comment floored her.

"You'll have to forgive him. He gets a little carried away with himself. But he does adore you."

Erica snorted to cover the fact that this conversation had already thrown her for loop. Trevor adored her? Yeah right. She opened the freezer and pulled out a tub of ice cream. After her latest incident with Trevor she decided to opt for cold and sweet instead of just sweet. The dim light was just enough for her to notice Jordan's grimace. She shut the door.

"If your definition of "adore" includes loving a boil on his backside, then perhaps you're right."

"You know it doesn't."

"Then I guess you're wrong."

"You know I'm not."

His casual observation had hope zinging through Erica. Then she thought of how she'd left Trevor upstairs. Never mind. Jordan handed her a spoon from a drawer near him and she took up the post nearby. She caught a whiff of apple pie which explained what he was doing down there.

"Sorry about the welcome I gave you earlier."

"Whatever. You hit like a girl." Erica heard the amusement in his voice so she didn't take offense.

"So do you." She dissected their earlier fight in her mind and how he'd seemed to be more powerful on his right side. That along with his sensitivity to light led her to ask, "Medical leave?" She took a bite of ice cream.

They stood in silence for a long time. She figured he wasn't going to answer her question. "Trevor's not going to be able to get anything by you, is he?" His question answered hers although it threw her back into the uncomfortable territory of talking about Trevor on a personal level. Especially since she knew he was talking about them on a more permanent basis.

"It won't be long before he won't have to worry about it." Erica shoveled in more ice cream.

"You're eating straight from the tub?"

"I'm going to finish it so why bother with a bowl?"

Jordan tested the weight of the ice cream in the tub and chuckled. "You are so family now."

Warmth rushed over her at his words. She tamped them down. He was just teasing. He pushed away from the sink and went to sit on a stool and looked at her. It seemed the position was painful for him because she was backlit by the security light outside. She also suspected that he wanted to look at her. His next question confirmed her suspicions.

"So how much trouble is my little brother in?"

Erica stayed in the light so he could see her body language while she relayed the truth of everything that had happened to Trevor. While she gave him the run down, he'd grunt every once in a while. Not long after she'd begun filling him in, he moved so he wouldn't have to look in the light anymore. That one little gesture of trust meant the world to her, especially after her mistake that had allowed Jordan to get to Trevor in his bedroom.

"And you're close to nailing the guy?"

"Anytime now."

Jordan nodded and continued to process what she'd told him. "Thank you," he said at last.

Erica almost choked on her ice cream. "Please don't. I've made so many mistakes . . . just. . ." She shrugged.

Jordan squeezed her shoulder. How was the man that quiet when he moved? "You've kept my brother alive. I know Trevor. He's not easy. Perhaps being in love with you kept him in check a bit, but still, thank you."

"He's not in love with me," Erica protested.

"If you say so." She heard Jordan's smile in his words. "If you ever get tired of the small agency, you should have Trevor hook you up with the Trecam Group."

Erica froze at the mention of her employer. "Why would I

do that? What does Trevor have to do with . . . ?"

"Trevor funds them. He'd probably kill me for telling you this. He has this weird hang up about having Trecam associated with him."

Erica could just make out Jordan's words over the roaring in her ears that began with 'Trevor funds them.' That couldn't be right. No way he . . . that would make him her boss for real. The boss that at that moment, she had handcuffed to a bed.

"He and Cam are silent partners. Cam's sister, Caitlyn, runs the joint."

"Really?" Erica couldn't believe that squeaky sound was her voice.

"Between Trevor and Cam, you'd have no problem getting in." With that last pronouncement Jordan left the kitchen. She was sure he didn't realize that he'd just destroyed her world.

* * * *

Erica spooned ice cream in her mouth on autopilot. It had lost all flavor a while ago. Trevor funded Trecam. He funded her life. Things fell into place. Like the huge chunk of Trevor's money she hadn't had time to track down to its ultimate destination. It had to have been going to Trecam. It paid her salary. It paid for their offices. It paid for that state of the art pool Caitlyn had commissioned once she came aboard. Crap. Did Trevor know?

She replayed their entire acquaintance in her mind and it settled on the safe house they'd used. The safe house that belonged to Trecam. She'd seen him in action long enough to know that there was nothing that went on in his finances that he didn't know about. He'd notice a house purchase. Her eternally optimistic side reasoned that maybe he hadn't recognized the address. That side was silenced when she recalled his strange behavior the next day. There was no doubt in Erica's mind. He knew she worked for Trecam.

The spoon scraped the bottom of the ice cream tub jarring Erica out of her troubled musings. She tossed the container and washed the spoon trying to delay her return to the bedroom for as long as possible. What in the world must he think of her? Did he assume she was this unprofessional with all of their clients like she'd been with him? Memory of the kiss they'd shared the previous night sprang to mind. She grimaced when she remembered how she'd hooked her leg around his hips drawing him closer, and then rejected him. And what about her constant antagonizing? And the way she'd bossed him around. She was so screwed.

Erica turned around to head for the door. Her steps slow like she was marching toward a firing squad. Whose wouldn't be? She'd handcuffed her boss to a bed. She'd threatened to tell his mother that they were having kinky sex. She'd blatantly admired his erection. She'd fallen in love with him. She pressed a hand to her reddening face. There was no good way out of this.

All too soon, she reached the doorway. She squatted to unhook the battery she'd wired to the doorknob. The jolt was less of a deterrent than an early warning system. Few people would be able to cover their noise of surprise when they touched the knob. Knowing she was delaying the inevitable, Erica opened the door and slipped inside the room.

Trevor was just like she'd left him. More or less. Sometime while she'd been gone, he'd untangled himself enough to drift off into a contented sleep. She was also glad to see his friend had relaxed, too. She stood and admired his inert form. With a gentle hand, Erica pulled the covers up over him and tucked him in. She pulled out the key to the handcuffs, but paused just before she released him. Another dilemma struck her.

There was nowhere else for her to sleep. And tonight, she had to get some rest. They were driving back to meet the crew tomorrow. She could slip into another bedroom, but she'd learned the hard way about leaving him alone.

Figuring she was already in trouble anyway, Erica tucked the key back in her pocket. She climbed in the bed beside Trevor and tried to relax even while clinging to the edge of the bed.

Chapter Fourteen

Erica was comfortable. Really comfortable. The most comfortable she'd been in quite some time. She was even rested. Rested and comfortable. A great combination. She opened one eye to see the sun streaming through the vertical blinds at the window and smiled. One should wake up to sunshine every day. No sooner had the notion surfaced, it went away. Something was wrong. She shouldn't be able to see the window. Not if she was still clinging to the edge of her side of the bed.

She opened both eyes and glanced around. Her worst fears were realized. Sometime during the night, Erica had draped herself all over Trevor like a cheap blanket. She looked up and saw his hand still cuffed to the headboard so she couldn't blame him. He was smiling down at her.

"G'morning."

Erica tried to push up, but she soon found that his free arm had circled around to hold her close. The hand of that arm had found its way inside the waistband of her sweatpants and panties and was resting very possessively on her bare hip. A hundred things popped into mind that she should say. Apologies. Explanations.

So she said, "This is behaving?"

Trevor smiled and angled his hand a tiny bit. His fingers brushed her most intimate curls. "All things considered, I think I'm showing quite a bit of restraint."

Erica grabbed his hand to stop any further exploration he may have in mind. "Your hand is inside my panties. How is that restraint?"

"Have you checked the location of all your limbs? Specifically your knee?"

Knowing she wouldn't like what she was about to find, Erica looked down. Somehow, she'd managed to free just enough of him from his pajama bottoms to give him an extremely intimate hug with the crook of her knee. Erica lost no time in straightening her leg to release him. She wanted to look a little longer, but her wits returned—along with the unwelcome memory that he was her boss. There was no doubt that this was inappropriate behavior.

"I'm so sorry." Erica sprang from the bed even though he tried to keep his grip on her.

"I'm not. It just proves my point." Trevor struggled to skooch up so he was sitting. Erica fished in her pockets for the key to the handcuffs. Not finding it, she knew a moment of panic. She tossed the covers back on the bed to continue the search. Trevor just watched, a puzzled frown on his face.

"It proves nothing."

At last, she located it under his thigh. With a triumphant pump of her fist, she unlocked the cuffs. Trevor raised an eyebrow.

"You almost lost the key?"

"The key was in my pocket until you decided to do some exploration."

Trevor rubbed his now free arm and stood. Erica scooted away to busy herself with removing the homemade alarm she wired to the window.

"I know you want to wait for us to talk, but things are progressing whether we want them to or not."

"Things are not progressing. In fact, there're no more things to progress." Erica put some distance between the two of them and packed the alarm back in her bag. It didn't take long for her to realize that she should've left him chained to the bed. He insisted on getting underfoot while she buzzed around the bedroom trying to keep space between them.

At last, Trevor gave up following her. He caught her in his arms and held her still. "What's wrong with you this morning? You're jumpy."

Erica refused to meet his eyes even though she could think of nothing better to do than drink her fill of his gorgeous eyes. "I'm not jumpy. There's a lot to do that's all."

Trevor looked at Lucy's Minnie Mouse clock. "It's barely ten thirty. We have plenty of time to get on the road."

"What do you want me to say, Trevor? I just sexually assaulted you and you want to pretend that everything is hunky dory?" She tried to pull away from him, but he held her still.

"What are you talking about? You didn't just—"

"Then what was that? That . . ." She gestured toward the bed. "I'm supposed to be protecting you. Who's going to protect you from me?"

Trevor laughed and tucked an errant strand of hair behind her ear. "You were asleep. Did you mean to assault me?"

"You know I didn't."

"And sexual assault has the connotation behind it that the advance was unwanted. You know much better than that, don't you?" He closed the distance between their bodies.

"You don't know what you want. I mean we've been cooped up together for almost six weeks. That's a long time to ask you to be celibate. Of course you'd respond to any stimulation." Erica broke free of his hold and walked away from him. His next words stopped her in her tracks.

"I've been celibate a lot longer than that, Erica." Surely he was kidding. He was always surrounded by women. How had he managed to . . . was he that controlled? And why did he relinquish that control around her?

"It's just . . . I see a lot doing what I do. I got desensitized. And it got old."

He gave her a crooked smile. One that in no way resembled his rock star one and just served to endear him to her all the more. Erica longed to tell him how much she loved him. But she couldn't get past him being her boss.

"Then you came along and it seems that I've turned into a horny teenager."

"I'm really sorry for breaking your streak, but it was bound to happen sooner or later." Erica withdrew her hand and paced to the window to put some space between them. If she didn't, she'd do something she knew she'd regret.

"It's you, Erica. There's no sooner or later about that."

* * * *

Trevor watched the emotions playing out over her face while he approached her. He didn't want to push, but he wanted her too much not to. And not just in a physical way. He'd realized at last why she was different. He'd fallen madly in love with her. Fallen? That implied time on the way down. He'd hit bottom the moment she'd tumbled into his life. Everything they'd gone through just made him love her all the more. She was a long haul kind of girl. His long haul kind of girl.

The thing about show business was that it was too easy to accumulate fake friends and hangers on. It was much harder to come by folk who looked out for you and weren't afraid to tell you when you were being a jackass. It was certainly a plus that she was gorgeous, but that wasn't all he wanted in a wife. He smiled in wonder. Erica Cole. That had a fantastic ring to it. Now he just had to convince her.

Yesterday, it seemed he'd made some progress, but today? She just stood there and stared at him with naked emotion in her eyes. Trevor stopped a hairs breadth away and waited for her to decide. Just when he could see in her eyes that he was going to like her decision, a phone rang.

All of a sudden, the look was gone and so was she. He turned to see her root through her bag with a look of near panic on her face. She found the phone and shoved it to her ear.

"Kellogg." Or maybe Kellogg-Cole, Trevor considered. This latest distraction was just that. A distraction. He wasn't about to give up. Not if it meant letting the woman of his dreams slip through his grasp.

* * * *

After listening for a moment, Erica stabbed a button to disconnect the call. She looked at Trevor and said, "We've gotta go." She noted the frown that crossed his face and the question in his eyes. "Now!"

She shoved everything back in her bag with reckless abandon then started to do the same with Trevor's. Everything he'd pulled out, she stuffed back in.

"We're going like this?"

Erica nodded. She didn't like it any more than he did especially considering that her bras were all in her bag and her breasts were pretty much just flopping in the breeze, but Jason told her that they'd lost the suspect not long after a celebrity Web site reported that Trevor was visiting his parents. While Jason and crew scrambled to find the guy, it was Erica's job to get Trevor back to town and into a safe house. Since Trecam didn't have its own tactical team, they relied on local law enforcement. At home they knew the locals would offer more protection than if they had to drag out credentials and explanations for cops they didn't know. As for his family, they would keep a watch on the ranch, but also issue a press release leaking Trevor's departure.

Trevor surprised Erica when he opened the door and picked up both of their bags. At her questioning look, he said, "You need your hands free, right?"

Erica nodded and led the way downstairs. Like she'd expected from the wonderful smells wafting through the house, Abigail was in the kitchen cooking. Jordan was sitting at the island watching his mother work. It appeared they'd interrupted their conversation when she and Trevor burst in. Abigail took one look at their bags and shook her head.

"Not on an empty stomach you don't."

Trevor put the bags down and gave his mom a big hug.

"Sorry Abby, we just got word of an emergency. We have to go," Erica tried to explain.

Abigail eyed them suspiciously. "You're not running off to elope are you? If so, I'll be ready in two shakes." She tried to break from Trevor who chuckled.

"Elope? I wouldn't do that to you, Ma."

"Then what's the rush?"

Trevor looked at Erica who was inching for the door. "A problem at the next venue. At this rate, the whole tour'll be cancelled. I need to go work it out."

Jordan eyed them throughout their production in silence.

Finally, he stood up and gave Erica a hug. "Should I stick around?" he whispered in her ear. Erica nodded and stepped back. They exchanged an understanding look before he pulled Trevor into a big hug. When the men parted, Jordan gave Erica a warning look.

"Take care of my little brother."

"You know I will." Jordan nodded and wrapped an arm around Abigail's shoulders so they could get away.

Trevor called over his shoulder, "Tell Dad we'll see him later."

"Go tend your business," Jordan growled in response.

Erica and Trevor hustled outside and threw their bags in the car. A few moments later, Erica had them barreling down the bumpy driveway while Abigail and Jordan waved from the porch.

Once on the highway, Erica pushed the car as fast as she safely could. She glanced at Trevor and was glad to note he didn't object to the speed. "Could you program the GPS?" she asked.

"Sure." She gave him the address while she searched for her Bluetooth in her bag in the back. He looked at her and stopped programming.

"Bluetooth?" Erica nodded and Trevor grabbed the bag to hand the headset to her before resuming his assigned task.

"Thanks." She slipped it on her ear.

He finished with the GPS and looked at her when she said nothing further. "So I take it we're not heading back for the tour."

She shook her head. "We need you to be in a location we can control."

"We?" He asked seeming puzzled.

Erica spared him a look. "C'mon, Trevor. We both know I'm not some one woman operation."

"We both know what?" He tried to continue the charade for a moment. Seeing she wasn't buying it, he shrugged. "So how'd you find out?"

"Jordan thinks I should ask you for a reference when this is over. He's fairly sure I'd get the job since you're one of the partners." Erica couldn't prevent the anger from bubbling up in her voice.

* * * *

Trevor glared at her. "So what's wrong with that?" He

frowned while a thought crossed his mind. "Wait. You're angry because . . . I never lied to you, Erica."

"Yeah, well you never came out and said 'I'm your boss' either!" Erica gritted her teeth. "Do you know how much better I could've done my job if I didn't have to keep hiding Trecam from you?"

"Ha!" Trevor shook his finger in the air. "So you admit that you're the one who did all the lying. So why are you mad at me? I should be mad at you."

"I was under orders to not tell you. What's your excuse?" Erica took her eyes off the road long enough to scowl at him. "Oh wait, you were too busy trying to seduce me. Me knowing that you are my boss woulda put a big ole crimp in your plans called 'sexual harassment!'"

"You are not serious," Trevor said once he could pry his jaw from his chest. He narrowed his eyes at her. "As I seem to recall, you were the one doing the sexual assaulting. Just this very morning in fact!"

Erica cringed then mustered up a bold smirk. "Where's your proof?"

"Oh. I'll have proof. I may have to manufacture it, but I'll have proof." He met her gaze and tried to keep the smile from surfacing on his lips while he heard what he'd just said.

He could see that Erica caught the expression and he sensed her own anger dissipating.

"I'll spin the most compelling tale of poor little me who just wanted to sing for people. Then along comes the big, bad bodyguard." He paused for dramatic effect and looked her over. "She's at least one hundred pounds lighter than me and a whole bunch shorter. She used her top secret bodyguard training on me and forced me to have relations with her. All night."

Erica laughed.

Trevor couldn't fight his smile anymore. "No, no. All week." He glanced at his wrist that was still raw. "She chained me up and made me do all kinds of wicked things. Totally against my will. It was horrible."

Camaraderie restored, they drove on. On the way to his parents', Erica made sure they'd arrived on a full tank of gas. Her caution had paid off since they'd been able to put quite a few miles between them and the ranch without needing to stop. The high speed guzzled the gas faster than normal so Erica had to pull off the highway, almost an hour from their destination according to the GPS.

When she stopped at the pump, Trevor reached for the handle to climb from the car without a second thought. She put a hand on his arm, stopping him. "I got it."

And he did, too. She didn't want him out in the open. Instead of arguing, he nodded and laid back in his seat.

* * * *

While Erica pumped the gas, the cool air seemed to flow right through her thin shirt. What a difference a few hundred miles north made! Without a bra, she knew her nipples were on display for all and sundry. Her suspicions were confirmed when a truck driver gave her a toothy grin and honked his horn. Thank God for pay at the pump.

She hunched her shoulders forward, but it didn't do much good in the form-fitting shirt. At last, she gave up. Pretended to be as brazen as all get out. She ignored the next few honks and climbed back in the car.

Trevor looked at her with a frown. "What's with all the racket? Oh." He grinned and stared with blatant interest at her chest.

Erica socked him with the back of her hand and started the car. "Eyes front."

"I kinda like them where they are."

Under his admiring stare, Erica had no hope of getting them to relax. She held her seatbelt away from her chest to prevent any further stimulation.

"Want me to get that for you?" Trevor's offer sounded innocent enough. One glance at his hot gaze told her otherwise.

"There's a burger joint over there. You hungry." She decided a diversion might be in order. Besides, the sight of the fast food place had her stomach growling.

Trevor never took his eyes off her. "I could eat."

Erica wisely didn't ask, "eat what?" She wheeled them into the drive thru. Less than fifteen minutes later, they were on their way again. Erica smiled to herself when she noted how Trevor seemed to forget all about her erect nipples once she'd thrust a hamburger in his hand. Guys were so easy.

He nodded to her chest. "I'll look forward to a repeat performance later."

Erica bit into her burger. Hard.

All too soon, Erica turned into the neighborhood that was their destination. She called Jason on speed dial and he opened the garage door for them remotely. When Erica eased the car to stop inside the garage she turned to look at Trevor. "Welcome to your new home." She climbed from the car. He followed a bit slower.

He addressed her over the top roof of the car. "How long am I supposed to stay in my . . . . new home?"

Erica pulled her bag from the car and headed for the door that led to the house. "A day. Two, tops."

Trevor looked at her skeptically. He could do a day. He had to get back to his tour. He grabbed his bag and followed her into the single story brick house.

* * * *

The day, two tops had stretched into a week and now Erica was frowning at him. She studied him and frowned the whole time he whipped up his world famous omelets for dinner. She'd frowned at him all day in stark contrast to the cheery country interior he'd grown thoroughly sick of seeing. He placed their plates on the kitchen island and sat on the stool across from her which had become their custom at meal times. He said grace, she added her scripture and he dug in. She kept staring. Unable to take anymore, he laid his fork down and met her look.

"What is it?"

"You're different."

Trevor laughed. "That's ridiculous," he lied. He'd never been better. After being cooped up for so long, he'd gone a bit stir crazy. He wanted to blame it on the gingham patterns he couldn't escape anywhere in the house, but he knew it was because they'd bonded on a whole new level giving

Trevor a glimpse of what life would be like married to her. And he liked what he saw. Respecting her enough to do things the old fashioned way, he'd put the brakes on trying to seduce her and went for making her fall in love with him. Sometimes he could see his success in her eyes which just made staying away from her physically that much harder. Seeing she had the same struggle made the task almost impossible.

To make matters worse, Erica had continued his swim lessons. The combination of seeing the pride in her eyes at his progress and her lack of dress made the attraction even more difficult to bear. So he'd done the one thing he could think to do. After she'd gone to sleep the night before, he snuck out of the house for a brisk run around the neighborhood. The run had worked so well, he couldn't wait for her to go to bed that night so he could slip out again. Since she'd flat out refused to let him go anywhere, he was keeping his nightly treks to himself.

"You've done something. What'd you do, Trevor?"

"You've been right here with me all day. Have you seen me do anything?"

Erica mulled over his words and gave in.

* * * *

Erica jerked awake, but lay still. She had no idea what pulled her so abruptly from slumber. Not that it had been all that peaceful. Her dreams had been filled with ways things could go wrong. She wasn't sure why. She and Trevor were safe stashed away while Trecam's top investigative team was working around the clock to locate Worthingham. Nothing would go wrong.

That was the last thought she had before a hand slammed down over her nose and mouth. She caught the sweet antiseptic odor of chloroform and held her breath. She'd be in trouble if the smell turned rotten. Knowing she couldn't last very long, Erica forced her body to go limp. Apparently satisfied that she was knocked out her attacker dragged her off the bed.

Feet free of the bed covers, Erica launched her attack. The man was caught off guard when she brought her foot up over her head to kick him in the face. Immediately, he released her. She had to get to Trevor. Erica sprung to her feet and headed for the hall. Her attacker snared one of her ankles and brought her crashing to the floor.

She kicked at him with the other foot. After landing two solid blows, he released her. She sprinted for Trevor's bedroom again. Surprise stopped her cold when she opened the door and noted the empty room. That was all the advantage her attacker needed. Erica felt something shatter against her skull then vaguely remembered hearing the thud her body made when it crumpled to the floor when everything went black.

Chapter Fifteen

Not long after he'd gotten outside, Trevor realized that the illicitness of his little escapes had worn off leaving behind nothing but guilt. Deciding to cut his second and last run short, he turned to head back to the safe house. When he rounded the corner, he knew in an instant that he was in deep trouble. Every light in the place was blazing. Erica had figured him out.

Feeling like he was heading toward the guillotine, Trevor forced himself onward. He practiced excuse after excuse in his head. He was almost at the door before he'd decided on one he liked that might have a snowball's chance in hell of working on her. Trevor pushed the door open, excuse all ready on his lips, and he froze in horror at the sight that greeted him.

Erica was sitting, more propped, on a chair in the middle of the living room. Her head rested in an awkward position on her shoulder and blood had just begun to dry on her shirt. Panic shot through him.

"Erica!" Trevor dashed toward her. His first instinct to free her.

She lifted her head a fraction and shook it. "Run."

Her voice was so quiet he almost didn't hear her. Run. Not

on her life. And not without her. He knelt at her side to free her hands and arms of the duct tape that bound her.

"Leave it, Mr. Cole."

Trevor's whole body froze. He looked at the man now standing between him and the door. When Trevor looked the man over, he had to admit he was surprised. The man was still a kid. Twenty at most. The pudgy little guy couldn't have been more than five feet tall. And that would've been on a good day. Judging by the bruise forming on his eye and his red, swollen nose, Trevor could tell today wasn't exactly that. He gave Erica's shoulder a proud squeeze.

"Edward Worthingham, I presume."

Edward glared at Trevor and slammed the door. He smoothed the brown peach fuzz on his chin and said, "You know who I am."

Trevor shook his head and shrugged. "Just hazarding a guess." Determining that the man couldn't be a real threat, Trevor reached to free Erica again. All of a sudden, he was shaking uncontrollably and dropped to the floor. A little drool slid from Trevor's mouth, but otherwise he couldn't move. Edward stood over him.

"I told you to leave it." Trevor's world went black.

Next thing he knew, Trevor was sitting, more or less, in an armchair. He could see Erica's worried expression from across the room and tried to give her a reassuring smile. The left side of his face wasn't working at the moment. Trevor tried to stand, but realized that his feet had been duct taped to the legs of the chair while his hands were bound in his lap.

"Mr. Cole. I'm so glad to see you're awake." Edward looked at the gunlike contraption he held. "I was beginning to think I hit you with too much juice."

"What'd you . . ." Trevor tried to ask, but his tongue was too thick.

"You'll be all right. For now." Edward put the Taser on the coffee table and sat on the sofa facing Trevor. The man casually crossed his legs like they were having a civilized visit.

"Wha d'you . . . What do you want?" Trevor had to concentrate on enunciating each word. Not the easiest thing to do. He could still feel tiny jolts of electricity sparking around in his body. Not the kind he got from being near Erica, either.

Edward smiled. "I'm so glad you asked. It's simple. I just want my money."

Trevor frowned. "Your . . . I don't have your money. I don't even know you."

"Not knowing me didn't stop you from stealing from me, did it?" Spittle flew from Edward's mouth like his rage got the best of him for a moment. He caught himself, relaxed and sat back again. "I've tried to be reasonable. I've asked you time and again to pay what you owe, but you wouldn't even take a meeting. Mr. High and Mighty. But I've got your attention now, don't I?"

"You crazy lunatic! I don't owe you a meeting and certainly don't owe you any cash." Trevor was fed up with this little game. From behind Edward, he could see Erica shaking her head, trying to get him to back off. The sight of her bound just made him that much angrier. "You're going to release us and turn yourself in to the police. You have a lot to answer for."

"As do you." Edward snatched the Taser from the table and swung it around to take aim at Erica. "I'll make you talk to me one way or another. Even if I have to torture your stupid girlfriend to do it."

"No!" Trevor yelled when he saw Edward's finger tightening on the trigger.

Edward cocked his head to the side. "What? You don't want to find out what happens when someone who's bound gets Tasered? I bet it'll be fun. She'd probably just snap a couple bones from the muscle twitches. No big deal."

"Look. Whatever you think I owe, I'll pay it. Just don't hurt her."

After a moment, Edward relaxed. He replaced the Taser on the coffee table and gave Trevor his full attention.

"I'm not trying to be unfair. Or even unreasonable. I just want what's mine."

"I understand. Just spell it out for me."

Edward crossed his legs and held up a finger. "First, I want ninety percent of all the income you received from albums sales of Nitetime. Next, I want seventy percent of your take from all royalties received from Nitetime. You can keep your tour revenue. Mostly. I want a twenty-five percent cut of every venue where you've performed Nitetime."

Trevor noticed Erica working on her bonds. He dragged his attention away and nodded. "I haven't been paid for the album sales or any royalties, yet, but as soon as I do . . ."

"Not good enough. I want it upfront. I'm sure you have an accountant who can project my cut."

"Yes, I do."

"In addition, I'm to be paid a monthly usage fee going forward for as long as the album remains in release." Edward leaned toward Trevor. "To be paid six months in advance. Do we understand each other?"

Trevor nodded. "I just have to call my accountant." Trevor held up his bound hands and smiled his rock star smile. "I kinda need these to put this in motion."

Edward glared at him. "No you don't. I'll hold the phone for you." He crossed to Trevor. "What's the number?"

Trevor looked at Erica. Edward was so close. If he could just . . . Erica was shaking her head like she'd read his mind. Edward nudged him. "The number?"

"Uh . . . I don't know . . . it's saved in my phone."

Edward's breath quickened when his anger resurfaced. "You wouldn't be trying to jerk me around would you?" His fingers tangled painfully in Trevor's hair and yanked his head back. "I don't want to kill an income source, but I will."

"I'm not jerking, I'm not!"

"I know the number!" Erica interjected. Trevor rolled his eyes down to see her. How would she? Edward abruptly let go of Trevor's hair and approached Erica.

"Nice try, sweetheart. A man doesn't trust his finances to a piece of ass."

Erica affected a ditzy tone. "No, but when I sees the writing on the wall that he's tired of me, I makes sure I have a nice parting gift."

Edward smiled. Looked back at Trevor. "Looks like you bedded the wrong chick." He turned his attention back to Erica. "What's the number, doll?"

While Erica rattled off a number that Trevor had never even heard of before he realized what she was doing. She was calling in the cavalry. God, he wanted to kiss her. He opted instead for working his hands loose. He was still sweating so much from that Taser blast that he should be able to slip free.

Erica recited instructions to Edward who figured she was giving him account numbers, but Trevor knew she was giving specifics about the situation. While Edward blindly aided in his own downfall, Trevor thought about how much he loved Erica. Now that rescue was on the way, Trevor was eager to get to their happy ever after.

Edward pulled the phone abruptly from his ear. "They want a passcode."

"Try fishes have fingers," Erica suggested.

Edward repeated the ridiculous phrase into the phone and waited. He covered the phone again and glared at Trevor. "You! You changed it!" Edward stalked back over to Trevor and shoved the phone in his face. "He says he needs the correct code in your voice so get to it!"

Trevor searched his suddenly blank mind. He didn't know any code. He looked to Erica. She mouthed, "Anything."

"Uh . . . the sparrows are walking."

Edward returned the phone to his ear and listened a bit longer. With each passing moment, his smile got larger and larger. He hung up the phone. "The sparrows are walking indeed. They'll call back in fifteen minutes to confirm the transfer and then I'm out of here."

"Why Nitetime? Is it your favorite or something?" Trevor couldn't resist asking.

"Well, I wrote it. Of course it's my favorite. It's far superior to your usual drivel."

Trevor frowned. "You are delusional. I wrote Nitetime last summer in Paris."

"Stop lying!" Edward screamed at Trevor and smacked him in the head.

"Trevor!" Erica tried scooting closer. "Just leave it alone."

"No way. I'm paying this guy a usage fee. I just wanna know what I get out of the deal." Trevor glared up at Edward. "Let me get this straight, I'm now paying you a fee to use my own work. That's rich."

"It's not your work and you know it! Or have you just gotten so caught up in the lie that even you don't remember the truth?"

"What is the truth? Tell me."

"I submitted that song to you personally right after I'd finished it. You stole it!"

"Neither me nor my people accept unsolicited work. I write my own music. End of story."

"But you . . . you took it! All you had to do was say no. Every time I called your office to ask for it back, they'd say they didn't know what I was talking about. Then you released the album. My track was the title track. You'd changed the name from One in a Tree, but I recognized it. An artist knows his own work."

"One in a Tree? What the . . . you actually think I'd even look at a song with that title?" Trevor laughed. "Seriously. One what in a tree? Why is it in a tree to begin with?"

"Enough, Trevor!"

"You're darn skippy. It is enough. This man has turned my life upside down. He's costing me money, right this second because I'm supposed to be on tour, but instead I'm tied to a chair and listening to him babble about me stealing his song about a tree!" Trevor's chest heaved with every angry breath he sucked in.

"You brought this on yourself. If you'd just given the napkin back . . . but no. You had to go record it. If you didn't want to pay me, you should've just let me sell it to someone else!" Edward leaned down to get in Trevor's face. "That song was my chance to show Mummy and Daddy I'm gainfully employed so they'd release my trust fund. And you Mr. High and Mighty Rock Star stole it from me while I have to make due with a paltry allowance! Who can live on a hundred grand a week anyway?"

"So let me piece this together. You wrote a song. On a napkin, no less, and expected to sell it? What was on the napkin? Lyrics? Music? What?"

"You know good and well it was the lyrics."

"So you're expecting a ninety percent cut of all the profits for a whole lot less than fifty percent of the work involved in getting the track produced?"

"Without my lyrics, that song is no good."

"Newsflash, bucko, no one even knows the lyrics. So even if you did write them, which you did not, they're not the reason the track sold. Even the music by itself ain't all that. It was the production that sent if off the charts. And I can assure you, my producer was paid quite well for his work." All his patience had run out with this nutjob. "And you actually believed you were going to break into the music industry with some song lyrics written on a napkin when there are tons of guys who are producing kick ass albums in the trunks of their cars who can't get their work into the hands of an A&R exec? I bet you can't even play an instrument."

Edward reared up. "I can too! I learned the recorder in fifth grade."

"What's the fifth flat in an E flat scale?"

"None of that matters now. Once I earn my first dollar, Daddy'll release the trust fund and I can retire."

"Retire? You're like twelve. You have nothing to retire from." Trevor nailed the kid with a hostile glare. "I almost wish I had stolen your pathetic little ditty. A loser like you wouldn't know what to do with it anyway."

With that, Edward's temper snapped. He dove at Trevor all flailing fists and battle cries. Erica could just sit there and watch.

"My God. Trevor! Get off of him!" she demanded and tried to hop her way into the fray.

Trevor's chair tumbled backward and Edward slapped him repeatedly. Trevor used his bound hands to ward off the blows the best he could, but he still took a couple slaps. At last, Edward tired himself out. He stood and straightened his jacket. He pressed a hand to his chest like he needed to steady his heart, then sat Trevor upright again and fixed his clothing.

"Guess you got nothing to say now."

Edward was just standing there, smirking at Trevor when his hand finally slid free of the tape. Trevor couldn't say who was more surprised. Him or Edward. Not waiting around, Trevor sprang from the chair to tackle the man. With his feet still taped to the chair's legs he couldn't get very far, but it was far enough. He felled their assailant like a sack of bricks.

Edward screamed like a banshee and tried to get to the Taser. Trevor held on to the man for all he was worth. The chair hindered Trevor's movement allowing Edward to get a grip on the weapon. The man fumbled, but got it under control. He aimed at Trevor and pulled the trigger.

Trevor tensed for the spasm he expected, but it never happened. He looked at Edward who was frowning at the thing. He shook it and pulled the trigger again. Trevor eased toward him.

"Stop!" Erica cried. "He didn't reload, but he can still Tase you once he figures it out."

Trevor nodded and worked at freeing his feet. He'd gotten one free when Edward's face lit up. "Aha!" He gripped the Taser and headed toward Trevor again. "Now let's see who the tough guy is."

"It won't be you. You had the advantage the whole time and you still haven't won." Trevor worked feverishly to free his other foot.

"Don't let him touch you with it," Erica warned while Edward approached Trevor. He spun on her and waved the Taser at her.

"Maybe I should shut you up first." Edward took one step toward her when Trevor got himself totally free. He launched himself through the air and tackled Edward from behind. The man smacked his head on the hardwood floor and lost his grip on the weapon. It slid out of his reach. Three punches had him dazed enough for Trevor to step back. Edward rolled into a fetal position and cried. Trevor picked up the Taser and went to free Erica.

"Are you okay?"

"I'm fine. You?" She checked him all over for injuries. She rubbed the mark the Taser left on his shoulder. "That'll probably scar."

He gave her a crooked smile. "Just make me that much sexier, right? Not that I need any help, though."

Erica shrugged and bent to untape her feet. Trevor'd expected a joke or something from her, but she was all business. Trevor didn't have time to ponder her standoffishness for much longer because Edward screamed and ran at them both again. Trevor picked up the Taser and held it so Edward ran into the prongs. The man dropped to the floor and convulsed with violent muscle spasms. Trevor watched dispassionately for a moment then continued to free Erica. Before he could check her injuries, the door burst open and cops swarmed the room.

They trained their guns on Trevor. "Drop the weapon!"

Erica held up her hands. "He's the hostage!" She pointed to Edward. "That's your kidnapper."

Jason stepped in with his own weapon drawn. He took in the situation. "She's one of us. He's her client."

The policemen lowered their rifles and handguns then proceeded to clean up the situation. The rest of the night and most of the early morning passed in a blur of giving statements and Edward crying about how he was robbed. When the excitement died down, Trevor realized he was alone. Erica was gone.

He rushed out of the house sure she was waiting for him outside. At the very least, she was his ride. Waiting at the curb instead was the guy who'd vouched for Erica when he'd first arrived. He was leaning casually against the hood of a black Mercedes with arms folded across his broad chest. Big mirrored sunglasses concealed most of his face, but his chiseled jaw was very much prominent. Especially while he chomped on a piece of gum. Erica worked with this dude every day? Trevor couldn't help straightening to his full height. Nothing, but the man's mouth moved when he said, "I'm your ride."

The two men climbed into the car. Once Trevor fastened his seatbelt, he ventured to ask, "Where's Erica?"

The other man gritted his teeth. Trevor would hate to be that poor gum. "She resigned."

His terse response had Trevor spinning to look at him. "What? Why?"

"She thinks she botched this case. Worthingham got to you."

"That's silly. He got in because I left. That was out of her control."

The irritated look the man gave Trevor left him no doubts how he felt on the subject. "All of us know that."

Trevor wisely let go of the conversation.

* * * *

Erica couldn't believe she was here. Hidden behind her very large sunglasses and humongous floppy hat, she scoped out the entire stadium. God it brought back memories. A smile creased her lips when she noted teams huddled in corners land drilling their routines. Some were near enough that she could hear them counting in unison.

Coaches surrounded the pool giving their soloists last minute instructions and running them through pool patterns. She cringed when she saw a couple swimmers almost collide in the pool while they worked their separate routines. Erica relaxed when she saw them each smile and apologize before continuing about their business. How many times had that happened to her? How many friends had she made at meets like this?

Her smile faded. Apparently not many or she wouldn't be an outsider looking in right now. She took another look around the stadium. There weren't many faces she recognized. Maybe that was a good thing. The fewer people she recognized meant the fewer people who would recognize her.

Then she saw her. Dani. Her old duet partner and her little entourage entered the stadium like they were royalty. Perhaps Dani was. After all, she was the sole Olympian Erica recognized. Judging by what she'd seen at practice, most of the people there competed more for fun than serious competition. In fact, she hadn't seen any real competition for Dani since she'd arrived that morning.

Erica watched Dani stroll around the pool like she was a queen surveying her peasant subjects. How pathetic was that? The way other swimmers deferred to her even going as far as to give up their seats on the bleachers annoyed Erica to no end.

When it came right down to it, Dani had never been the most technically sound swimmer. If Erica was honest, the girl had coasted on her coattails. But somehow between the entourages and awed deference, it was obvious the woman had forgotten that fact. Too bad Erica hadn't brought a suit.

Erica shook off the fantasy of showing Dani up when the referee cleared the pool to begin the competition. Erica lost herself in the excitement of the routines. Both the excellent and the not so hot.

She eavesdropped on the people around her when they told the story of the current swimmer who if rumors could be believed taught herself how to swim off the Internet just a couple years ago. She'd picked up synchro a few months later and here she was. Her absolute joy at being in the pool was obvious and her smile lit up the stadium. Erica remembered those days for her and a twinge of jealousy hit. She shook it off to continue watching and was impressed with the girl's verticals. They were all very high and straight. Erica could tell she was a new swimmer, but it was obvious she was a fast study.

Erica was so engrossed in the current routine that she didn't notice the woman who sat beside her until she leaned in to whisper, "I don't know about none of this stuff so you're gonna have to talk me through it."

Erica sucked in a surprised breath and looked at Megan who was squinting at the action in the pool. "What are you doing here?"

Megan pointed at the swimmer and her eyes lit up. "Oooh! Oooh! I've seen you do that. What's that called?"

Erica looked back at the pool in time to catch the tail end of a familiar hybrid. One she'd made up years ago. She smiled. The girl must have studied her. Erica sure liked the kid's gumption. She was going to make sure she said hello to her before she left. "It's an old hybrid."

Megan heard the wistfulness in Erica's tone. "How come you're not out there? You know you want to?"

"It's a competition. I'm not registered."

"I'm sure they'd make an exception if someone were to tell them who you are." Erica looked at Megan in alarm.

"You didn't."

"No. But he might have." Megan nodded across the pool where Trevor stood staring at her. Every single one of her emotions seemed to flood her at once. How much she loved him. Her anger that he'd almost gotten them killed. How much she missed him. Her frustrations that she was now out of a job and he'd forbidden anybody to give her references. How good he looked.

"Oh my God. No. I can't go out there. I . . . I . . . ." Erica searched her mind for any excuse she could think of. She knew once Trevor flashed that smile of his, any referee would throw in an exhibition in two shakes. "I don't even have a suit."

Without a word, Megan thrust a gorgeous green suit at her. The crystals and sequins formed elaborate patterns that could only be handmade. Erica looked at Megan in awe. "This is . . ."

"Are you going to let all that work go to waste?"

Erica laughed. "So now you're blackmailing me."

"Absolutely." Megan cast a critical eye at the suit. "Come back when you get it on. I want to make sure it's a perfect fit."

"It will be." Erica hugged Megan and climbed from the

stands. She paused and looked back at her. "But tell me why. I'm not . . ."

"You're family. We don't let family go that easily."

Determined to not let Megan see her cry, Erica turned and fled for the locker room. It took no time for Erica to change into Megan's suit and matching cap. While Erica checked it out in the mirror, she saw that it was an exquisite fit. Megan was a miracle worker with a needle and some thread. She smoothed the suit over her backside as she turned and met Dani's angry eyes in the mirror.

"What are you doing here?" Dani demanded and stalked toward her.

"I'm swimming an exhibition," Erica explained in a conciliatory tone. "I didn't ask to, it just happened."

"I bet. Like it just happened that you couldn't be bothered to show up at the Olympics." Dani got in Erica's face. "Do you even realize how much people here hate you? You cost this country a medal. They shouldn't have even allowed you to come back." With that pronouncement, Dani shoved her nose in the air and stormed from the locker room.

Erica stood in stunned silence. Other swimmers were all around them staring and not bothering to hide the fact they were listening to their argument. More than one of them that Erica didn't even know glared at her like she'd hurt them personally. Seeing that made something in Erica snap. She was tired of cowering behind one little mistake that incidentally saved Dani's life.

"Anyone have a nose clip I can borrow?" More than one swimmer followed Dani's lead and left the locker room. Others turned away without a word and went about their business.

"I have one," a lone voice said behind her.

Erica turned to see the new swimmer she'd just watched holding out a nose clip. Erica smiled gratefully and took it. "Thanks."

The girl blushed and shrugged. "Keep it. It's the least I can do since I've borrowed some of your hybrids."

Erica laughed. "And you do them very well."

The girl lit up at the compliment. Erica nodded at her, then followed Dani from the locker room determined to finish this once and for all.

Erica scanned the pool deck and found Dani waiting for her

routine to be announced. She noticed that the woman wasn't even wet. She was so smug that she hadn't even bothered to warm up. A plan began to form in Erica's mind.

Dani's number was called. The queen was back. She walked to the center at the edge of the pool and did her deck work. Erica couldn't believe it. She was going to swim their duet as a solo. The woman couldn't even come up with a new routine.

Trevor came over to Erica. "Erica . . ."

"Don't let them stop the music," she told him while she scrubbed her nose on the suit and put on the nose clip.

"What?"

"The sound system is over there." Erica pointed then ran and dove in the pool. Trevor scrambled to the scoring tent.

Dani's face was livid when Erica surfaced beside her and performed the routine as a duet.

"What the hell are you doing?" She put her arm down.

"Are you afraid I'll show you up? With your own routine, no less," Erica challenged. She watched Dani's eyes dart around the stadium. She got back on track with the next one count.

Erica and Dani finally swam their duet, but it wasn't like either of them ever imagined. Instead of competing against other teams, they were battling each other. Every figure had to be more precise. Every hybrid had to be more extended. Every boost had to be higher. Every eggbeater had to be stronger than the other person's in the pool.

Halfway through the routine, Erica could tell that Dani was getting winded. Even though she was still competing, it was obvious she hadn't stayed in as good a shape. Then again, considering the competition, she hadn't needed to.

During the slower middle section of the music, they had a long sequence above the water. Erica figured she and Dani could talk then.

"I've told you a million times how sorry I am about missing the competition."

"Shove it . . . up . . . your . . . rear. Swim!" Dani was almost gasping for breath and her smile was looking pretty forced. Erica put more pressure on her and sped up. Not wanting to be shown up, Dani struggled to keep up.

"I'm finished apologizing, Dani. I'm finished with listening to your snide remarks. I'm done being afraid to swim simply because you are." They went underwater for another quick hybrid and a direction change.

"I didn't blow the competition off that day like you've been telling anyone who'd listen. It hurts that after all the time we spent together that you would think that of me."

"I'm not . . . listening." She was really starting to pant now.

"Whatever. That loser boyfriend of yours tried to blow you up. Unfortunately, I triggered the bomb instead. I had to stand there, not moving a muscle while Interpol diffused it. That's why I missed the events. Since I saved your life, I'd think you'd cut me some frigging slack!"

"I don't . . . believe . . ."

"I don't care. Just know that I'm back. You're no longer the lone big fish in this small pond." To prove her point, Erica sailed through the remainder of the routine. She literally left Dani in her wake. Erica even added the more exciting hybrid to the end of the routine that they'd had to take out when Dani was never able to get it.

When the music stopped there was dead silence in the stadium. Erica and Dani swam to different ladders to exit the pool. She paused to watch her old duet partner climb onto the deck. Erica was sorry that things couldn't be fixed between them, but she knew it was time to let it go.

Trevor started clapping and cheering Erica on. She heard Megan join him, the applause built around the stadium until it turned into a standing ovation. All were looking at Erica. Dani slunk off to the locker room with only half of her two swimmer entourage. The other girl didn't even notice when they walked off.

Erica took a moment to enjoy the cheering audience. She was home. Where she belonged. All thanks to Trevor. She looked for him on the deck and was surprised to see he'd stripped down to some swim trunks. She paused, one hand on the ladder, wondering what he was up to.

He stared at the water for a long moment then jumped in. Erica sucked in a surprised breath and swam back out to where he'd splashed down. What was he thinking? She hadn't worked him up to water this deep yet. She was just about to dive down to find him when he surfaced nearby.

"What are you doing?" Erica caught his arm and tried to hold him steady. His legs were flapping back and forth trying to hold his head above water.

"It looked like you needed a new duet partner." He offered her a toothy grin. It was brief because he forgot to kick and went under again.

Erica laughed and pulled him back to the surface. "First, you've got a lot to learn."

He suddenly turned serious. "I know. And I want you to teach me. Every day. For the rest of our lives."

Erica inhaled and backed away a bit. What was he saying? Trevor doggy paddled after her. "See? I'm at least a little trainable."

"I don't know what to say, Trevor."

"Just say yes." He stopped paddling with one arm to reach into his pocket. His head went under again.

"Trevor!" Erica hurried to catch him and push him back up.

The water didn't even seem to faze him. He shook the drops out of his eyes and held out a three carat round cut diamond ring with baguettes surrounding the center stone.

"You told me to wait until I didn't need you to see if I needed you. I do. I want to show you how much for the rest of our days. Marry me, Erica."

"I'm not going back to Trecam," Erica warned. Caitlyn had been quite persistent in trying to woo her back.

"I'm not here for Trecam. I'm here for you." Trevor set his jaw stubbornly. "And I'm prepared to hound you until you say yes. So, what's it gonna be?"

"Is that a threat?" Erica asked. She couldn't keep her amusement from shining in her eyes.

"Try promise."

A smile burst forth on Erica's lips despite her tears of joy and she kissed him. Like she'd expected, the familiar jolt of electricity zinged through her. She could tell it zinged through him, too, if the sudden press against her belly was any indication. Now she was home. The thought faded when Trevor pulled away to look at her.

"I'm afraid I need an answer."

She leaned in for another kiss and whispered against his lips, "Yes. My answer is yes."

Trevor let out a whoop and sank again. With a laugh, Erica pulled him back up. He slid the ring on her finger and kissed her again. Erica smiled when he pressed against her harder and harder.

Finally noticing the applauding crowd, Trevor whispered, "Um, Erica, how are you planning to get me out of this pool without everybody knowing our business?" She laughed and swum him toward the shallow end of the pool so he could stand while he regained some control.

Even though people swarmed them to offer congratulations and compliments on Erica's amazing swim, their problem was still pressing against her hip.

She turned to Trevor with a twinkle in her eye. "I think we're going to need a short engagement," she said with a twinkle in her eye.

Trevor grimaced. "Best idea you've had all day!"

The End

About the Author

Lori Crawford has two great passions—television and writing. As a child, she was a walking TV guide. When not watching TV, she was devouring every book she could get her hands on. Nearly a decade later, her love for reading developed into a passion for writing. She graduated from short stories and imaginary friends to write her first novel when she turned sixteen. It went on to languish in the bottom of a drawer where it rightfully belongs. She is delighted to share this novel with you which is waaaayyy better than the first one.

Printed in Great Britain
by Amazon.co.uk, Ltd.,
Marston Gate.